Praise for

Cassidy Ryan

From beginning to end, this story swept me along on a pleasant buzz of adrenaline and anticipation... Once the case was cracked, it revealed an interesting twist that connected Hal and Luke in an unexpected way. While satisfied with the ending, I'd love to see a sequel with more of Hal, Luke and especially Milo. Hmmm, seems like the start of their own little pack! Very much enjoyed this one!! ~ *Hearts on Fire*

The plot is very engaging... I also adore their loving scenes. They were absolutely brilliant with the visceral passion and eroticism of such relationship all there for me to taste and breathe...In the end, this was a most satisfying story I enjoyed very, very much. One I would love to see a sequel of, as there were plenty characters and possibilities for follow-ups. Totally recommended. ~ *MM Good Book Reviews*

A well written well paced arousing romance...a splendidly engaging saga that I thoroughly enjoyed. ~ *Literary Nymphs Reviews*

Total-E-Bound Publishing books by Cassidy Ryan:

Bound by Love
Aria
Cadence
Imperfect
Truth and Beauty

KISS OF THE WHITE WOLF

CASSIDY RYAN

Kiss of the White Wolf
ISBN # 978-1-78184-622-3
©Copyright Cassidy Ryan 2013
Cover Art by Posh Gosh ©Copyright April 2013
Interior text design by Claire Siemaszkiewicz
Total-E-Bound Publishing

Published in 2013 by Total-E-Bound Publishing, Think Tank, Ruston Way, Lincoln, LN6 7FL, United Kingdom.

Total-E-Bound Publishing is an imprint of Total-E-Ntwined Limited.

KISS OF THE
WHITE WOLF

Dedication

With huge thanks to my editor, Rebecca, and my
beta-reader, Josie.
You keep me on my toes and make me look good.

Chapter One

And the truth shall set you free.

How many times in my thirty one years had I heard that phrase, or variations of it? When I was a young boy I told my baby cousin Amy that dog biscuits were people food too. Confessing to my mum meant no pudding after dinner and an early bed time, rather than the week without television that would have been the consequence of any attempt at deception.

As an adult, truth was the tenet upon which I built my journalism career. It was the right of the people, the foundation of democracy.

I had no idea that it would also be the catalyst for events that would turn my life upside down and inside out, bringing about some of my worst and best days.

It started simply enough. I was working for a top national newspaper when I got an anonymous tip that a Metropolitan police officer was taking money to influence the outcome of investigations—The Farmer, they called him, because of his ability to plant evidence. It had been a slow news week, so I decided to do a bit of poking around.

Within weeks I'd discovered that The Farmer was just the tip of the iceberg. Informants were crawling out of the woodwork with their tales of corruption, intimidation—convictions and acquittals bought and paid for. Unfortunately, none of these informants were willing to go on the record, and my editor was starting to get agitated at my failure to produce.

I couldn't let it go, though. In my gut I knew I was onto something. There was a cartel of officers in the Metropolitan Police Force selling their services to the highest bidder. *Robbed a bank, but don't feel like going to prison? No problem, bung us a few grand and we'll bring you a patsy to hang the blame on.* Men had gone to prison for crimes they hadn't committed while the real offenders, often violent, dangerous individuals, went about their crooked business with impunity. I just couldn't fucking prove it.

After two months, my editor finally lost patience and issued his ultimatum—bring the story home or clear my desk. I still didn't have cast iron proof, and if we were going to avoid a potentially crippling law suit, I would need nothing less. But I'd already invested so much time and energy, and I was loathe to see it all wasted.

In the spirit of truth and honesty, I have to admit there was an element of stubbornness verging on obsession in my decision to resign and go it alone. I won't deny that I felt a little trepidation at working for the first time without the safety net provided by being an employee of a media giant. But there was also a kind of exhilaration to be found in the uncertainty of the path I'd chosen to walk.

For many more months I continued to dig, surviving on my rapidly dwindling savings as I visited prisons around the country, interviewed countless inmates, their friends, families and even their criminal connections, for few of these men were entirely innocent. Most of them were 'known to police', some particularly distasteful, and probably deserved to be in prison at one time or another. But the fact remained that, this time, they'd been incarcerated for something they hadn't done because of a small group of police officers who, for the sake of some nicer suits and faster cars, had chosen to betray the people's trust and pervert the laws they had once pledged to defend.

The breakthrough I so desperately needed came in the form of Charlie Speight, a career villain from London's east end. When he contacted me, Charlie was in his sixties, suffering from end stage lung cancer and eager to leave his mark before he died.

Charlie was an old-time safe cracker who had managed to always stay two steps ahead of the law. The light of Charlie's life had been his son, Steven, a university graduate on his way to a doctorate in, of all things, criminology. Charlie had determinedly kept Steven distanced from his own life, wanting something more for his son. Unfortunately, Charlie's ability to avoid arrest had made something of a fool of the police, and over the years the resultant resentment had festered in one officer in particular – Detective Chief Inspector John Stoke.

While looking for someone to take the fall for an armed diamond robbery, Stoke had seized his chance to settle the score with Charlie, fitting Steven up so neatly that it had taken the jury less than an hour to find him guilty. Steven's life sentence had infuriated his father. The young man's suicide just months later took the heart and soul out of Charlie.

For the next four years, Charlie devoted his life to putting together a dossier of the misconduct of Stoke and his cohorts—comprehensive details of banks accounts and property held under fake identities, photos and recordings, both audio and video, of meetings with criminal clients to arrange plans and payoffs. He'd intended to turn over his findings to the press, but when he'd heard, through the underground grapevine, about my own investigation, he'd called and asked me to meet him at a café in Lambeth. Over bacon sandwiches and strong, black tea he'd told me his story, then had handed over the thick file wrapped in brown paper and string.

It was a journalist's wet dream. And a publisher's too, apparently, judging by the bidding war my agent gleefully presided over.

Charlie was there at the book launch, grinning like a loon in spite of the fact that he could barely stand up unaided. I sat with him in the hospital during his final days, and we watched the news reports about the arrests of seven Metropolitan police officers, the highest ranking of which was DCI John Stoke. Charlie's laughter was wheezy and ragged, but no less joyful for it. He died before I got the chance to tell him that the book had hit the top of the bestseller list.

In the months that followed, I rather envied Charlie's absence from the world, as my own life seemed to implode.

I'd foolishly assumed that once the promotional obligations were over—the TV and radio chat shows, the book signings and readings, magazine and newspaper interviews—things would go back to the way they had been before, when I had been happily anonymous—the one who wrote the headlines but was never the subject of them.

What I got instead was hack reporters camped out on my doorstep, paparazzi shoving cameras in my face at the supermarket, and glossy magazines wanting to do 'at home with' photo shoots, like those of minor celebs lounging around their bedrooms in the latest Armani or Dolce garb.

I made the mistake, late one night, of calling the police when I came home and found some scumbag reporter going through my desk drawers. Long after I hung up the phone I could still hear the cop on the other end laughing.

My former editor offered me my old job back, with a 'significant pay rise'. I told him I'd get back to him once all the nonsense had died down a bit. I *wanted* to tell him to shove his job and his pay rise up his arse, but my dad had taught me early that you should never burn bridges just in case you have the need to cross them again.

When it became nigh on impossible to pop out to the corner shop, unmolested, for a pint of milk, I decided that I had to get away from it all for a bit. A wild weekend in Brighton was just what I needed—plenty of booze, loud clubs and hot guys.

I arrived on Friday evening, booked into a hotel and sprawled, fully clothed on my king-size canopy bed, already feeling more relaxed than I had in weeks, and drifted off wondering what I should do first. When I awoke, still in the same position, in the same clothes, it was Saturday afternoon and I felt no desire to be anywhere else. I ordered a burger and a beer from room service, took a quick shower then dressed in my boxers and a T-shirt. I piled the pillows up in bed, lounged back against them, and watched a *Dirty Harry* marathon on the big screen TV while I ate. Just before film three started I called back to room service and had them send up an ice cream sundae with strawberry sauce.

It wasn't the weekend I had planned, by any stretch of the imagination, but, by the time I checked out on Sunday afternoon, I felt refreshed and ready for another round.

* * * *

If I'd chosen to stick to the main roads—the A23 and the M23—I could have been home in just over an hour and a half, but it was a lovely, crisp November afternoon, and I was in no hurry to be anywhere, so I stayed on the quieter country roads. Also, I'd only recently bought an Alfa Romeo and was enjoying being behind the wheel of my first brand new car.

I took a meandering path, cracked the window just enough to let in the fresh scent of late autumn, and turned the music up until I could feel the thumping beat of it in my chest. I encountered very little traffic, with the notable exception of a couple of dozen motorcyclists riding in convoy, all wearing the same hi-vis yellow jackets with what looked like a flower on the front.

At a few minutes after four I passed a sign for Caterham, in Surrey, and my stomach rumbled, reminding me that I hadn't eaten anything since the toast and jam I'd had with tea that morning. I considered taking a quick detour to see if I could find a pub serving food, but I was less than an hour from home, and it was already dark, so I decided to keep going and pick up some take away instead.

A couple of miles along the road—a narrow, winding road illuminated only by my headlights—I was singing along to Adele on the MP3 player, off-key and unembarrassed, when something in my peripheral vision caught my attention. The words of the song froze on my lips, my head snapped round to the right and I scanned the treeline at the side of the road, but saw nothing. My pulse thumping a little too fast for comfort, I turned back to the road, only to notice that I'd swerved over to the wrong side. With a muttered curse, I righted the car, grateful that there were no other vehicles in sight. I glanced in the rear-view mirror before I took the next bend, and my heart seemed to stutter and stop even as I slammed my foot down on the brake pedal.

In the red glow of the rear lights, I watched as a man, clad only in what looked like a pair of black boxer briefs, appeared from the trees to my right, hurried across the road in a wavering, uneven gait, and stumbled onto the grass verge opposite. He dropped to his knees and appeared to be having some difficulty getting back up. Every ounce of common sense in my body told me to stay in the car, get the hell out of there. But as the thought was forming I found that I was opening the door.

A blast of cold air hit me and I shivered. I could only imagine how this semi-naked stranger must feel. He'd be damn lucky if he didn't have frost bite.

After turning off the music, I got out of the car. I grabbed and pocketed the keys, then closed the door, just in case this was some kind of car-jacking scam. When I got to the back of the car, the guy was still trying to push himself to his feet, and I caught the sound of low, angry curses coming from his direction.

"Hey, are you all right there?" I asked, drawing slowly closer.

His head jerked around in my direction, face partially obscured from view by tangled, shoulder length hair that I guessed to be blond, but the car lights gave it a red tint. "No!" he seemed to growl, and his voice had a raw edge to it. He dragged himself upright with no little effort and turned towards me. "You stay there. Don't come any closer."

I was near enough that I could see him a bit better now. He was tall, taller even than my own six-two, and he was big with it, broad across the shoulders and chest with powerful looking, muscular arms and legs. In another situation, perhaps in one of those clubs in Brighton, I would have explored the heat that suddenly burned low in my gut, but at that moment concern overwhelmed all other sensation, even the fear that continued to prickle along my spine.

"I just want to help you," I said, trying to make my tone as reassuring as possible. I raised my hands in front of me, palms up. "Will you let me help you?"

For the beat of a few seconds there was silence. His shoulders drooped and he shifted one foot behind him. Believing that he had accepted I was no threat to him, I took another step forwards and smiled, as much in relief as encouragement. But before the toe of my boot even touched the ground he was moving, lips pulled back in a snarl as a roar of sheer rage tore through the darkness.

I could only watch, frozen and horrified, as he bounded towards me, as though unleashed, in a display of energy and grace that, just minutes before, I wouldn't have imagined him capable of.

Every breath of air left my lungs in an explosive *whoosh* when he collided with me, his shoulder to my chest. I must have flown six feet backwards before I landed with enough force to make me wonder, fleetingly, if I would ever draw breath again. My head glanced against the hard surface of the road, leaving me dazed, and it was a struggle to open my eyes. I did so just in time to see him bearing down on me.

"Don't..." That was all I managed to get out before his massive hand closed around my throat, fingers squeezing until I felt my head would surely pop. Panic seized me and I pushed frantically at his shoulders, tried to work my knee between our bodies to give me a bit more leverage. But he was too big, too strong, and in his pale eyes I saw a glint of steely determination.

"I won't go back," he declared, and I felt the words rumble from his chest to mine. "Do you hear me? I won't let you take me back there."

Chapter Two

My vision was beginning to blur around the edges. I scrabbled at his bare shoulders with frantic fingers, my nails digging into his cold skin. Despite my efforts he continued to throttle me, eyes flashing, breathing in short, sharp gusts.

"S-stop, please." My words were practically inaudible and seemed to have no effect on him. My eyes felt like they were bulging out of my skull. Was this it? Was this to be my end, strangled on some lonely country road by a near-feral mad man?

Fear-induced adrenaline coursed through me, lending some clarity to my oxygen deprived brain, and I noticed for the first time the gash on his shoulder, mere inches from where I'd been scratching. Even in the poor light provided by the car's headlamps, the wound looked open and raw. Without a second thought I slipped my hand closer and dug my thumb into the injury with as much force as I could muster.

A howl of indignation erupted from my assailant and he pulled back just enough to allow me to roll to the side, out of his reach. I managed to scramble a bit farther away and get to my knees, ignoring the burn of fabric against my skin and keeping him in my line of vision the entire time. What would we look like, I wondered, to any motorist who happened to pass at that moment—me, struggling to breathe through a throat that felt like I had a bad case of tonsillitis, sagging as the energy began to drain from my body now that the immediate danger had passed, and him, crouched on all fours like an animal waiting to pounce.

"Please," I said again, hoping to stall him before he could go in for the kill. "I-I really don't want to hurt you. I'm sorry about your shoulder, but please believe me, I just want to help." *Dear God, make him believe me,* I thought. I could see the power practically vibrating through him, could still feel it in the ghostly imprint on my neck.

His eyes narrowed and his head tilted slightly to the side as he seemed to consider me. After a long moment, during which time my heart was beating so fast it was making me lightheaded, he said, "You're not one of them." It sounded like equal parts question and statement.

"I don't know who *they* are," I replied, sitting back on my heels in a deliberate attempt to appear non-threatening. "My name is Hal, Hal Paxton. What's your name?"

He regarded me for another few seconds, but with relief I saw some of the tension leave his body and he sank back until his position mirrored my own. "Luke, my name is Luke. You're not one of them," he repeated, this time very definitely a statement.

"I'm not." I shook my head and let my gaze move over him. It was with some shock that I saw that the shoulder wound was not the only injury he bore. The skin over his ribs was discoloured and he had a cut and a dark bruise around his cheekbone, partially hidden by hair that looked in need of a good wash. Congealed blood had gathered along his hairline and there were countless other abrasions and wounds over his arms and legs. But what made the breath catch in my sore throat were the deep grooves in each of his wrists, the skin there abraded and bleeding. He had been tied up, and by the looks of things there had been no kindness shown to him. Concern rose to the surface again. "I think you need a doctor, Luke."

"No, no doctor, I want... I just want...home." He sagged, as if his own adrenaline rush was wearing off. "I want to go home."

I nodded. "Okay, your choice. Where do you live? I can take you there." I think if he'd said he lived in the Highlands of Scotland, I would still happily have driven him home that night.

His eyelids drooped and he seemed to have to think about it. "Hertfordshire, I live in Hertfordshire."

"Well, that's not too far away." I smiled and began to get to my feet. The movement made him flinch, and from one second to the next he was all coiled tension again. I pointed to the car as I continued to slowly rise. "I'm just going to get you a blanket, okay, Luke? You must be freezing out here."

He looked down at himself then, and his brow furrowed, as if only now realising that he was practically naked. I frowned too. He appeared to be disorientated. Was he hypothermic?

I fetched the tartan blanket from the back of the car and brought it to him. He was still sitting there, but now he was just staring at his hands. "Come on, Luke, let's get you in the car, eh? I've got the heat up quite high, so you'll thaw out in no time." I draped the blanket over his shoulders, and, with my hands on his upper arms, I urged him to his feet. He was surprisingly accommodating now, and that bothered me more, I think, than another violent outburst might have.

Once at the car, I opened the passenger side door and gestured for Luke to get in, but he was suddenly still, his body stiff and uncooperative.

I moved so that he could see my face in the light from the interior. "Luke, I promise you, I'm not trying to trick you or hurt you. I just want to help, okay?"

When he turned his head and his eyes met mine, I saw no fear or trepidation there, but there was definite reluctance in his expression. "I-I don't want to mess up your car." He looked down at his feet and my eyes followed. A gasp escaped me before I could stop it. He looked like he'd been walking over broken glass, the skin torn and bleeding.

I looked at his face and my heart contracted. He was a mountain of a man, and I'd already witnessed the ferocity of his temper, but right then he looked for all the world like a little boy who was worried he was in trouble.

"Don't worry about it," I said softly, trying to coax him in with a hand at his back. "It will clean easily enough."

He looked a little doubtful, but got in, shivering when the warmth from the heater surrounded him. I closed the door and rounded the front of the Alfa to get in the other side. He was slumped in the seat, and looked tired, but I noticed he was resting his feet on their sides so as to make as little contact with the floor mat as possible.

"I'm going to fasten your seat belt, okay, Luke?" I asked, and waited for him to nod before I reached over him to retrieve it. I clicked it into place, and when I lifted my head I found that he was watching me intently. A tendril of heat uncurled low in my belly, but I doggedly ignored it and set about fastening my own seat belt.

"Hal," he said. I looked over at him. His eyelids were heavy, his lashes, thick and dark, brushing against the tops of his cheeks.

"Yes?" I asked, glad to have the excuse of the sore throat for the rough sound of the word.

"I'm sorry I hurt you," he replied, and brought a hand up to lightly touch the side of my neck. I felt that touch all the way to my toes. "You're very pretty," he added, as his eyes closed and his hand fell away.

For a brief moment, alarm widened my eyes and my pulse kicked up again, until I noticed that his chest was moving in deep, even breaths. I smiled, relieved and flattered, and tucked the blanket tighter around him before I started the car.

I got onto the main road at the first opportunity, and drove in near-silence for nearly an hour, Luke's soft breathing replacing the music of earlier. When we were nearing the outskirts of London and Luke was still sleeping, I reluctantly decided I was going to have to rouse him, in order to get directions to his home. I said his name a few times, quietly at first, then louder when he didn't respond. When he slept on, I put a hand on his arm and gave him a shake, but that too failed to wake him. A sudden feeling of disquiet crept up on me, and I pulled the car over to the side of the road and turned to Luke. His head had fallen to the side and his hands lay lax on either side of his thighs. I lifted one of his hands and tapped the back of it sharply—not enough to hurt, but enough to get the attention of even the deepest sleeper. Luke didn't so much as flinch.

"Oh, *shit*, come on, Luke, let me see those baby blues." I tamped down resurgent panic, fumbled my seatbelt loose and turned in my seat. I could still hear Luke's soft exhalations of breath, and his chest was moving in a steady rhythm, but there was no reaction of any kind when I slapped his cheek a couple of times, and when I lifted his eyelids his pupils were completely unresponsive to the light.

I slammed my hand against the steering wheel with a harsh curse and reached for my phone. My fingers trembled on the keypad, but I soon had directions to the nearest hospital with an emergency department. I sent up a prayer of thanks that it was less than twenty minutes away and pulled the car back out into traffic.

The lights of the hospital were like a beacon, guiding me in from a mile out. When I pulled the car over as close to the emergency department as I could get, I barely took the time to turn off the engine before I was out and running.

"I need some help!" I burst through the doors and skidded to a halt in front of the reception desk. "Please, I need some help."

The woman behind the desk was, I guessed, creeping up on middle age, and was clearly used to such dramatics. Her bland expression didn't change as she regarded me over the tops of her glasses. "What's the problem?"

I gestured wildly back over my shoulder, and the man passing behind me ducked in time to avoid losing an eye. "My-uh, my friend, he's in the car…unconscious. I can't get him to wake up."

The woman raised an eyebrow at me, as if to ask, *isn't that what unconscious usually means*? But she turned and picked up the phone beside her. "Where is the car parked?"

"Right outside," I replied, and Jesus, my heart was going like the clappers. But at least if I was having a heart attack I was in the right place.

She said something into the phone, but I was too busy looking over my shoulder to hear what. "How about you? Are you okay?" she asked when she replaced the receiver, and her gaze fell pointedly to my neck. I guessed that I must be starting to bruise already.

"Fine, I'm fine, can you just..." The double doors at the side of the reception area opened then, and two scrubs-clad men appeared, pushing a trolley.

Relief flooded me, and I ran outside ahead of them. I felt worse than useless as they loaded Luke onto the trolley and rushed him back inside. I stayed close the whole time, but when we reached the doors beside reception again, one of the men turned to me.

"I'm sorry, but you can't come any farther right now. Perhaps you can give Mrs Cooke some information while we look after your friend?" He didn't wait for my reply, but let the doors swing closed between us.

I stood there for a moment, watching the doors until they stopped swinging, then turned back to the reception desk where the triage nurse, Mrs Cooke, was waiting with an expectant tilt to her head. What the hell was I supposed to tell her? I'd already told the others the sum total of what I knew about Luke — his first name. But she was still watching me, so I returned to the desk, pulling the collar of my jacket closer to my neck as I did.

"Fill this in, please," Mrs Cooke said, holding out a clipboard and a cheap biro. "Give us as much information as you can, it will help the doctor treat your friend faster."

I rubbed a hand over my face, wishing that my pulse and heart rate would get back to normal, right the hell *now*. "I-I can't, I don't actually know him, I just kind of...*found* him and he collapsed...kind of."

Both eyebrows went up this time and she set the clipboard back on the desk. "You found him. So, not your friend then?"

I felt my face heat with a flush. This woman reminded me a little too much of every teacher I'd ever had. "Not exactly, no."

"Well then, isn't that a thing? Nevertheless, the doctor might want to speak to you about the young man's condition when you *found* him, so if you wouldn't mind taking a seat?" She pointed at the waiting area with the Biro, and it was very clearly *not* a request. "After you move your car from the entrance, of course. There's a car park just around the corner."

I just nodded and did as I had been told, certain that she inspired such reactions in everyone she met.

When I'd moved the car and returned, I took a seat with the dozen or so other people waiting, some of them nursing injuries, others drinking tea from paper cups and flicking absently through old magazines.

I'd been waiting for maybe a couple of hours, alternating between staring at the floor and the swing doors, and deliberately not making eye contact with Mrs Cooke, when a shadow fell across me. I glanced up and saw the two police officers looming over me, standing closer than was strictly necessary.

"You the one who brought Mr Tallis in?" asked the elder of the two.

I blinked a few times. "Mr Tallis?"

"Luke Tallis." The detective, a short man somewhere in his forties, with thinning hair and bags under his eyes, held out a police warrant card with his photograph on it. "I'm Detective Sergeant Childes. The nurse at reception said you brought the unconscious man in." He didn't bother to introduce his colleague.

Luke *Tallis*. How did they know...? My eyes widened and I sprang to my feet. "He's awake, then?"

Childes took a step back and frowned. "I believe so. Perhaps we could have a word in private." Without waiting for my assent, he turned and led the way to a door marked '*Staff Only*'. The young constable said nothing, but gestured for me to go ahead of him. I was aware of him following behind us, his rubber-soled shoes squeaking on the floor.

"I don't have all the details yet, but I believe Mr Tallis is in quite a bad way," Childes said, crossing the small office to perch on the corner of a utilitarian desk. The door closed and I looked over my shoulder to find the constable standing in front of it, hands behind his back. "Could you tell me how you came to find Mr Tallis?"

Bad way? What exactly did that mean? Surely if Luke was awake enough to talk then things couldn't be that bad? Tension coiled afresh in my stomach and my hands clenched at my sides. I gave Childes the truncated version of how I had come across Luke — leaving out the part where he'd tried to strangle me, because it appeared his situation was crap enough without me getting him in trouble for assault.

Childes nodded as he scribbled in a small notebook. "And, what's your name, sir?" he asked, without looking up.

Dread settled like a weight on my shoulders. Of course they would need to know my name, it was standard practice in any kind of investigation. I could only hope... "Hal Paxton," I said, aware of the hint of defiance in my voice.

There was a moment of silence as Childes seemed to raise his head in slow motion. Something like a smile lifted the corners of his mouth, though it held no humour. "Well, now, PC Devlin, it appears we're in the company of a celebrity."

Devlin's only response was a derisive snort. The sudden contempt flying between the two men was thick enough to taste. It was the kind of reaction I'd been getting from officers of the law since the publication of my book. Childes pushed up off the desk and took a step towards me, smile morphing into a sneer. I supposed it was meant to be intimidating, but the man was a foot shorter than me, and I'd faced down tougher than him — cops and crooks.

"Why are you here, Detective? Who called you in?" I asked, belatedly, and perhaps to move the attention from myself for a bit.

Childes seemed to consider whether or not to answer my question for a moment, before saying, "The medical staff were concerned at Mr Tallis' condition. They called in a possible assault."

A quiet knock at the door spared me the venom I could see rising in the detective's eyes. When I turned, PC Devlin had opened the door to admit a pretty young woman. Since every medical professional had taken to wearing scrubs I found it difficult to tell who was a nurse, who was a doctor and who was a porter.

"Detective, the doctor has a moment to speak with you now," she said in that gentle tone that seemed unique to healers.

"Thank you, nurse," Childes said, heading out of the room. Before he vanished from sight he added, "You'll keep our friend company, won't you, PC?"

Devlin closed the door again with a loud click, then folded his arms over his chest. He looked like a fucking nightclub bouncer.

"Actually, I need to use the loo." I smiled as pleasantly as I could, and nodded at the door. "If you'll just excuse me?"

His eyes narrowed and he stiffened, but he moved aside to let me pass. I closed the door behind me before he could follow, and looked along the hallway for the toilets. Instead I saw Childes and the nurse turning a corner a few yards away. The pressure on my bladder decreased in direct proportion to a surge of curiosity — the driving force of any journalist.

Glancing around to make sure that PC Devlin hadn't chosen to accompany me, I hurried in the direction in which I'd seen Childes go. I paused at the corner and peered out cautiously. Childes was standing just a few feet away, and the nurse had been replaced by an older woman in darker scrubs. She flipped through the papers attached to a clipboard until she found the one she was searching for.

"Mr Tallis has extensive bruising and lacerations, a couple of wounds that required stitching, and several electrical burns from what I would guess to be a stun gun of some sort, but nothing of major concern...at least physically. He does, however, have massive doses of barbiturates in his system," she said, eyebrows pulled together in a frown. "Under...normal circumstances we would be talking overdose and calling the morgue."

"Normal circumstances?" Childes asked, and though he was standing with his back to me, I could hear his scowl in the tone of his voice. "Please explain, Doctor."

The doctor sighed and held the clipboard against her chest. "Mr Tallis' system appears to be metabolising the drugs at an accelerated rate. Now, I'm by no means an expert on the matter, but I believe this can be explained by his werewolf genes."

Her words seemed to explode in my head. Werewolf genes... Luke had werewolf genes. That would mean... Luke was a *werewolf*? Jesus Christ on a pogo stick. My stomach felt like it had plummeted to settle somewhere around my ankles. My legs felt suddenly too weak to hold me upright, and my head was spinning. I slumped back against the wall and closed my eyes.

Chapter Three

"A *werewolf*? Are you kidding?" Childes sounded nearly as stunned as I felt. "There hasn't been a werewolf sighting in the UK in years."

The doctor emitted a delicate snorting sound. "Yes, well, they were hardly welcomed with open arms when they tried to integrate, were they? Who can blame them for retreating back into anonymity after the fiasco of the millennium?"

My befogged brain processed her words like an antiquated computer, but it didn't take much digging to recover the memory of that time. A group of wolf shifters had decided that it was time for their kind to step out of the shadows, to confirm the rumours of their existence and take their place in the world. Humanity's reaction had been laughably predictable—fear and aggression.

There had been demands for disclosure and enrolment on a public register, protests in the streets, clashes between anti-were and pro-were factions and, ultimately, the far more insidious actions of the fascistic Prime Order organisation. It was like stepping back into darker times—attacks on werekind that ranged from distasteful propaganda to sickening violence and even murder.

Retreating back into anonymity was one way of putting it. Driven into hiding in fear for their lives and those of their children was much more accurate. The activities of Prime Order were quickly brought to a halt, but the damage was already done.

Luke would likely have been a teenager back then. What must it have been like for him, to witness such hatred, to listen as his people were described as 'barely evolved' and 'inherently bestial'?

I recalled the gentleness in his eyes, the soft touch of his fingers on my neck and the quiet sincerity in his voice when he'd whispered, "Hal, I'm sorry I hurt you" and my chest ached. I'd taken part in a few marches for shifter rights when I had been at university, but, although I'd genuinely believed in it back then, it was only in that moment, with the image of Luke in my mind, that it finally felt real.

"When can I speak to him?" Childes' voice broke into my thoughts.

The doctor sighed. She sounded tired, and I imagined her pushing a hand through her dark hair. "Honestly, I don't know how much help it would be to speak to him right now. As well as the barbiturates, we found traces of flunitrazepam in his system. As a result, Mr Tallis has no memory of what happened to him. His memory may or may not come back—it's impossible to tell at this point."

"Fluni-whatsit?" Childes asked.

I was starting to feel sick. Flunitrazepam was also known as—

"Rohypnol," the doctor said.

My gut churned unpleasantly, and water brash filled my mouth. Jesus…

"*Rohypnol*. You mean the date rape drug?" Childes asked, clearly puzzled. "So, was he sexually assaulted?"

"There are no signs of that," the doctor replied, and my knees actually went out from under me with relief.

I slid down the wall and landed with a bump on my arse. *Thank God.*

"But something bad happened to this young man," the doctor continued. "So I'll let you in to talk to him, but please, go easy."

"Sure," Childes replied. "I can do that, but can you guarantee he'll go easy on me? Y'know." He made a growling sound, like an angry dog.

"The drugs appear to have suppressed Mr Tallis' shifting abilities, at least for the time being. Why don't you have a seat in the waiting room and I'll let you know when you can see Luke?" Her tone was cool, and when she passed me by, I heard her mutter "Arsehole."

I scrambled to my feet and caught up with her. "Excuse me, doctor."

She turned, one eyebrow arched, and I wondered if she was related to Mrs Cooke. "May I help you?" There was a flicker of recognition in her eyes when she looked at me. I'd been getting that look a lot lately.

"Uh, yes, I brought Luke in, Luke Tallis? He's awake now?" Probably best if she didn't know I'd been eavesdropping on her conversation with Childes.

Her expression seemed to lighten. "You must be Hal. Hmm, he *said* you were pretty. I thought it was just the drugs talking, but apparently not."

My cheeks heated, but I wasn't sure if it was embarrassment or pleasure. "He's going to be all right?" I found that her answer really mattered to me.

"He should be fine after a couple of days rest." She seemed to consider something before she spoke again. "Would you like to see him? It might be nice for him to have a friendly face present when he talks with that detective."

I was nodding even before she'd stopped speaking.

"Okay, come with me," she said, and continued down the hallway. I followed her through the doors beside reception and past several treatment rooms to the end of the corridor. "I'll bring the detective along in a moment. Perhaps you could make sure he doesn't upset Luke?"

"Of course, thank you."

When she left, I opened the door and stepped into the room. Luke was resting on a narrow bed, leaning back against a few pillows and covered by a starched white sheet. His hair had been pushed back from his face and the bruise on his cheekbone stood out in stark relief against the white of the gauze covering the cut there.

"Hi, how are you feeling?" I asked, and winced. How was he *feeling*? He was bruised, battered and drugged, and I was asking how he was *feeling*? Shit!

He looked tired, but when he smiled it seemed to light up his face. He seemed genuinely pleased to see me, and that did all kinds of weird, tingly things to my body. "Better than a few hours ago. Thank you for your help. Are you okay?" He lifted a hand to indicate my neck.

"Oh, I've had worse love bites." I laughed, moving to stand behind the chair by the bed.

"Is that right?" he asked, and the glint of interest that entered his eyes made me shiver. I curled my fingers into the plastic of the chair because I really wanted to reach out and touch him.

I recalled, for a flash, the weight of him on top of me, and my body responded instantly, heating, hardening. My mind screamed about the inappropriateness of that, but my body wasn't listening. "So, the, uh, the doctor said you should be good to go in a couple of days."

He grinned, and a dimple appeared in his left cheek. I wanted to lick it more than I wanted to fucking breathe. "I'm tempted to say something about being good to go right now, but that would be crass and kind of sleazy."

Thank God for that chair. I was harder than I could remember being in a long time, and he was all laid out in bed, mischief dancing in his eyes. It was difficult to remember that he was drugged and quite possibly not in his right mind. But still, I couldn't have stopped my next words if my bloody life had depended on it. "I've never been averse to a little crass and sleazy."

"I'll have to remember that," he said, his voice a low rumble. I clutched that chair so tightly my fingers hurt.

"Mr Paxton, I'd like to have a word with Mr Tallis, if you wouldn't mind waiting outside." Childes' voice was like a thousand icy-cold showers. The need that had been rushing through my veins came to a crashing halt and my erection began to wilt. The man was a better passion killer than bad breath. I had no problem turning away from the cover of the chair.

"I have the doctor's permission to be here, Detective."

Childes stepped into the room and pointedly held the door open. "Nevertheless…"

"I want him to stay," Luke interrupted. "I want you to leave. I have nothing to say to the police."

Wait, what? My head snapped around. "Luke? Somebody hurt you—you can't let them just get away with it."

Luke frowned. "I believe that's my choice. I want this to be over with, and I want to go home." The finality in his voice made it clear that he didn't want an argument.

But how could I just let it go at that? Okay, so I hadn't exactly saved the guy's life, but I felt this irrational sense of…*responsibility* to him that I couldn't begin to explain.

"Are you sure about this, Mr Tallis?" Childes asked, but he was already tucking his notebook back into his pocket.

Luke rested his head back against the pillows and turned his attention to the ceiling. "Positive."

I watched, dumbfounded, as Childes took a business card from his pocket, crossed the room and laid it on the bedside cabinet. "My number, in case you change your mind," he said, then headed back towards the door.

"Are you serious? That's it?" I demanded before he could leave.

Childes stopped in the doorway and glanced back over his shoulder. I'm certain I didn't imagine the hint of spiteful pleasure in the look he gave me. "Mr Paxton, I'm sure you know enough about police procedure to know that I can't proceed with an investigation without a formal complaint. I can't force Mr Tallis to make a statement."

Annoyance made my head buzz. "I don't believe this, you heard what the doctor said—something bad happened to Luke, how can you just *leave*?"

"I wasn't aware that *you* had heard what the doctor said," he retorted, but I was too irritated to feel abashed at getting caught.

"Well, I *did* hear, everything you heard. And now you're just going to walk away, do nothing?"

Childes shrugged. The fucker actually shrugged. "If that's the way Mr Tallis wants it."

Incensed, I took a step closer to him. "This is completely unacceptable, Childes."

"So, write a book about it," he bit out between gritted teeth, then turned his back on me and left.

I spun around, already building up to a rant, but my ire rapidly petered out when I was met with Luke's intent gaze. He had moved and was now sitting on the side of the bed, bare legs showing under the inadequate hospital gown. There were bruises up and down his shins, and his feet had been cleaned and bandaged.

"That wasn't necessary," he said quietly, his expression unreadable.

Fuck. Awkward. "Ah, I-I'm sorry, I'm afraid I got a little carried away. I...do that," I finished with a self-conscious shrug. *Stupid bloody journalist, can't keep your nose out of other peoples' business.*

Luke shook his head. "Don't worry about it."

"No, seriously, I'm sorry." I moved closer, embarrassment clawing at me. "I had no right...you said no, I should have kept my mouth shut. I have trouble with that sometimes, keeping my mouth shut."

"Really? I didn't notice." It took a moment for me to notice that his lips were twitching at the corners. By which time I wanted to find a hole to crawl into.

"Sorry," I repeated, and the word was barely more than a whisper.

"Hal, I'm not angry with you," he said softly, tilting his head slightly to the side. "Actually, it was sort of nice. It's been a long time since I had anyone in my corner. Thank you."

A smile tugged at my mouth. "Well, you're welcome." I felt ridiculously pleased.

He looked down at his hands, clenched them into fists before flexing his fingers. "Can I ask you something, Hal?"

Anything, I wanted to say, and damn if I didn't fucking mean it. Instead I made my voice as casual as possible. "Sure. What do you need to know?"

For a minute he was so quiet, still looking at his hands, that I thought perhaps he'd changed his mind. Then he lifted his head, and the eyes that met mine were steady and penetrating. "You said you heard the doctor say something bad had happened to me. What else did you hear?"

I knew what he was asking, of course, but his blank expression gave me no clue as to how he would react if I told him the truth. However, he deserved no less than total honesty, so I held his gaze and answered, "Everything."

"Ah." He nodded. He didn't look like he wanted to hurt me in any way. Promising. "And?" he added.

"And?" What did one say in a situation like this? *Sorry you got drugged and possibly beaten, but congratulations on being a werewolf?* "Uh, well… I'm not sure what to say. Maybe you could give me a clue?"

I wasn't expecting him to laugh. It was a rich, vibrant sound that seemed to resonate through my body. "Generally when people encounter a werewolf there isn't a lot of talking, just running and screaming." The mirth in his eyes seemed genuine, but I was certain I detected a trace of solemnity behind it.

Wanting to chase that away, I smiled. "I've been sitting on a hard plastic chair for hours—my legs are too numb to run, and I only scream under very specific circumstances."

"While I for one would love to hear just what those circumstances might be," the doctor said, entering the room silently on her Crocs. "I'm afraid it will have to wait until I get Luke settled in a nice, semi-private room for the night."

Luke's good humour faded in an instant. "A room? Why?" He got down from the bed to tower over the doctor, but if it was intended to intimidate, the wince he gave when his feet hit the floor spoilt the effect.

"I want to keep you in for the night, just to make sure there are no after effects of the drugs." She held up a white plastic wristband. "I brought jewellery."

Luke moved his arm out of the way when she tried to slip the ID band on. "I don't need to stay in, I feel fine. The drugs are already wearing off and the cuts and bruises will be gone in a day or two."

Setting her clipboard down on the bed, the doctor sighed. "I would really prefer that you stay, Luke, as a purely precautionary measure. I simply don't know enough about your physiology to feel at all comfortable letting you leave so soon."

"I do," Luke replied, and he seemed to be trying to reassure her. "I can feel the drugs leaving my system, and, as with all werewolves, the physical injuries will heal quickly."

"All the same, I think it would be prudent if you let us monitor you overnight."

I had to agree with her, but I managed to keep my opinion to myself this time.

Luke, however, shook his head firmly. "If you really want to help, you'll find me something to wear so that I can get home without being arrested for indecency."

"Are you always this stubborn?" she asked, but there was no heat in her tone.

He grinned, unrepentant. "I'm an Alpha—it's part of the package."

"An Alpha?" I asked, when the doctor had left us alone. "That means you're head of your pack?"

Luke's smile faded. "It means I was born to be." He turned away and I guessed that was the only explanation he was willing—or able—to give right then.

Chapter Four

The doctor — Rayburn — her badge read, provided Luke with a set of pale green scrubs that were a little too tight, but displayed the firm curve of his arse to perfection, and a pair of cheap plastic shower shoes.

"You're sure I can't talk you out of this?" she asked, in a last ditch attempt to change his mind.

Luke's only reply was a small smile.

Dr Rayburn sighed and shook her head. "Very well, but I want you to promise that you'll come back if you experience any symptoms that cause you any concern whatsoever, yes?"

"On my honour," Luke replied, laying a hand over his heart, and biting back a smirk.

She shook her head again, but I could tell that she was fighting her own amusement. "Fine, but get some rest at least." She handed him the clipboard and a pen to sign his discharge papers, then turned over the white plastic bag containing his personal belongings, which, in Luke's case, consisted of the blanket I had wrapped around him. She was muttering something about stubborn bloody men when she left.

"Come on, I'll take you home," I said, gesturing for him to precede me out of the room.

Luke hesitated. "Are you sure you don't mind? I've taken up so much of your time already."

I would have liked to have attributed my motivation to the simple desire to help someone in need, but in truth, I wasn't yet ready to part company with Luke. "I don't mind at all," I assured him, and was rewarded with a wide smile that made my insides do a funny little flip.

Insisting that Luke wait in the warmth of the waiting room, I brought the car around to the front and made sure the heat was turned up high. When he got in, I asked for his address and programmed it into the Sat Nav.

The journey took less than thirty minutes and for a while Luke was cheerful and talkative. But about twenty minutes in, he became quiet, staring thoughtfully out of the side window. I wondered what he was thinking about. Then I recalled what he'd said when he'd had his hands around my throat, *'I'll kill you before I let you take me back there'*. In all the activity and, yes, anxiety, I hadn't thought about it before, but it occurred to me now that he must have *some* memory of what had happened to him. What did he remember? And why hadn't he told the police? I was a little surprised to find that my curiosity felt much more personal than the kind of detached inquisitiveness I knew in my professional life.

On another quiet country road, I brought the car to a halt outside a set of iron gates. "This is home?" I asked Luke, squinting through the windscreen into the darkness beyond. All I saw were the gates, the high stone wall anchoring them and the shadowy outlines of trees.

Luke nodded and reached for the door handle. "I'll get the gates."

"No, let me." I put my hand out to stop him and accidentally made contact with his arm. His skin was considerably warmer now, and I couldn't help noticing how big and solid his biceps were. *Dear God, in other circumstances…* "You, uh, you stay warm."

His soft laugh sounded indulgent. "Hal, I'm fine. Besides, I need to key in a code to open the gates without the infra-red thingy." There was no wince this time when he got to his feet, so I guessed he wasn't exaggerating when he'd told Dr Rayburn that he would heal quickly.

The gates swung open smoothly and Luke got back into the car. "They'll close automatically behind us."

Gravel crunched under the wheels as I guided the car along the driveway and came to a stop again, this time in front of a white house with Virginia creeper clinging to the walls. I'm not sure what I'd been expecting—I didn't know nearly enough about Luke to make assumptions about him. But if I'd had to guess where he lived I would never have placed him here, in what looked like a family home.

But hadn't I been making a huge assumption about him without even thinking about it? Maybe he had a family, a wife and kids? The house was dark and quiet, but that meant nothing, really. The idea left a bitter taste in my mouth.

"Will you come in?" Luke asked quietly. "You've done so much for me, the least I can do is feed you."

It was well after nine and I'd still only had that toast for breakfast. My stomach had been rumbling pretty consistently the whole drive, so there was no point in denying that I was indeed hungry. "Won't we be disturbing anyone?" I asked, unable to quite meet his eyes. The question felt heavy on my tongue. I feared the answer, should it be the one I didn't want to hear, would weigh even heavier on my chest.

"I live alone," Luke answered, then opened the door to the cold air. "Come on inside."

I nodded, turned the engine off, then got out.

"Just give me a sec, I keep a spare key for emergencies," he said before disappearing around the side of the house. He reappeared a moment later with a smile, dangling a key ring from his index finger.

I pulled my jacket closer against the chill while he stepped onto the wide entrance porch and unlocked the door, then beckoned me forward. A wave of warmth washed over me as soon as I entered the house.

"Thankfully, the heating is on a timer," Luke explained, flicking a switch on the wall and bathing the area around us in light. I glanced around and found that the reception hall in which we were standing was quite spacious, but the exposed beams and brickwork gave it an intimate, welcoming feel. "The kitchen's this way, and rest assured, there's always plenty of food in my pantry. The appetites of a werewolf are best not neglected—we can become rather…snappish."

Did he hear me gulp when he winked? It certainly seemed loud to my own ears. "I'll remember that," I said, then flushed at the sidelong smirk he sent my way. Damn, when exactly had I become a blushing virgin?

He turned on more lights as I followed him along the hallway into a kitchen that looked like something from the pages of *Country Life*. Copper pots hung over a marble-topped island in the middle of the room, floral printed tiles lined the walls behind limed oak cupboards, and an entire wall was taken up with some kind of cooking range that looked frighteningly complicated. All it needed was the smell of fresh baked bread to add to the image of domestic perfection.

"This is nice," I said, feeling the need to say *something*.

He crossed the ceramic tiled floor to a retro-designed fridge then opened the door, smiling at me over the top. "But?"

"But?"

The dimple appeared in his cheek as the smile deepened and I found I had to suppress a groan. What was it with that damn thing anyway? I'd seen men with dimples before, but I'd never experienced this intense desire to explore them with my lips and tongue.

"I heard a but there," Luke replied, pinning me with those strange, pale blue eyes. "'This is nice...*but*...'"

"Oh, no, no but, just..." I shrugged, giving in. "It just doesn't seem very *you*. Although, of course, I'm probably completely wrong, given that I've known you for all of five hours."

Luke laughed and ducked into the fridge, taking out a carton of milk. "Actually, you're right, it's not me. I'm just renting the house. Oh, look, the milk's still good, so I haven't been gone that long."

The words were like a dash of freezing water. "You don't know how long you were...gone?"

He set the milk down on the worktop and returned to the fridge. "What day is it?"

"It's Sunday." I frowned and annoyance curled through me. "Didn't they tell you at the hospital? They should have asked you questions, to make sure you weren't, I don't know, *brain damaged* or something."

Luke retrieved some eggs and cheese this time, still smiling in that soft way that made me feel oddly like I was being *enjoyed*. "They asked me all sorts of things—my name, date of birth, who the Prime Minister was. They seemed fairly satisfied that there was no brain damage."

"So, how long have you been gone?" I asked.

His eyebrows pulled together as he seemed to think about it. "Well, I went into London on Wednesday to order some supplies for my work, then...then I went for a coffee while my car was in the garage to have the tyres checked for winter—*fuck*, where the hell is my car?"

"Wednesday? You've been gone since *Wednesday*?" I demanded, moving closer without thinking about it.

Luke nodded. "Hmm, yes, I believe so."

I rounded the island to stand before him, near enough that I could feel the warmth of him. "Luke, what happened to you? I know about the drugs, but you do remember some things, don't you?"

His eyes seemed to cloud over and he touched one of the bandages around his wrists. I couldn't, didn't *want* to, fight the need to touch him. I took a step closer and laid a hand on his arm in silent encouragement.

"I...I don't recall much after coffee. I left the café, and the next thing I remember is waking up. My head hurt and I was cold—my clothes were gone." He spoke slowly, as if he was having to drag the recollections to the surface. "Everything's so vague. I hear other people, men. I feel pain, like bright flashes. They're laughing, they find my pain funny. I'm angry, but…dulled. I couldn't shift. I *can't* shift." He sucked in a deep breath and shuddered.

My heart contracted at the anguish in his eyes. "It's the drugs, barbiturates and Rohypnol. The doctor said they're suppressing your abilities. But they're already wearing off, aren't they?"

The laugh that he gave was unexpected, soft but genuine. Unexpected also, was the hand that he lifted to cup my cheek. "You really did hear everything, didn't you? I feel like I had a protector when I was at my most vulnerable."

I couldn't stop myself from leaning into the gentle caress. My whole body seemed to tingle with awareness at his touch. "I-I don't quite understand it myself, but I couldn't just leave you there, alone," I admitted.

"Thank you," he whispered, and smoothed his thumb over my cheekbone before letting his hand fall away. "How about a cheese omelette?"

"Cheese omelette?" The words bounced around in my head like a pinball trying to find a target. "You want to make me an omelette?"

"You don't like omelettes?" He held up the box of eggs, then the lump of cheddar. "Or is it cheese? You don't like cheese?"

"No, it's…it's…" Jesus, I made my fucking living with words, but one touch from this man and I had the communication skills of an emo teenager. I guessed my smile to be the very definition of sheepish. "A cheese omelette would be great, thanks."

"Okay then." He grinned and began opening cupboards, taking out bowls and pans and far more utensils than could possibly be needed for such a simple meal.

As I leaned against the island and watched him work, an imp of mischief poked at me. "I didn't know werewolves cooked. Don't you prefer your food raw and *bloody*?"

He snickered and cracked six eggs into the bowl. "It's even better if it has a pulse." He emitted a little growl and lifted the corner of his lip to show a flash of incisor. It was surprisingly hot.

"Big bad wolf," I teased.

Luke stopped mixing the eggs, turned his head and gave me a rather pensive look. "You're really not afraid, are you?" There was just a hint of wonder in his tone.

The simple fact was that no, I wasn't afraid, not of Luke. But *why* wasn't I afraid, or at least mildly concerned? For all I knew, the pulse thing wasn't a joke, and the minute he was able to shift again might be my last. I racked my brain, but I couldn't come up with an explanation. I removed my jacket and laid it on the island. "You're making me eggs, if you were fattening me up for the kill there would at least be cake."

His delighted laughter filled the kitchen and danced along my nerves. "I'm glad Fate threw me into your path, Hal Paxton."

I found I heartily agreed with the sentiment.

When the food was ready we sat on bar stools at the island to eat.

"Will you have a beer?" Luke asked, moving once more to the fridge.

I shook my head and swallowed a bite of the very tasty omelette. "Thanks, but no, I have to drive."

Glancing at the school clock on the wall, Luke's brow furrowed. "It's after ten, you should stay the night."

It was a good thing I wasn't eating at that moment. As it was, I was having trouble not swallowing my own tongue. "Stay?" The word sounded strangled.

Luke laughed again and pulled two bottles of Stella Artois from the fridge. "I promise not to ravish you in your sleep." He opened the bottles and set one in front of me, then resumed his seat opposite me.

Well, that was a tad disappointing. "I feel I should argue, but in all honesty I wasn't looking forward to driving again tonight, so thanks, I'll take you up on your offer." I raised my bottle in a toast, smiling when he clinked his against it.

We ate in easy silence for a while, and I stole glances at him between bites of food. I guessed him to be somewhere in his late twenties, and very handsome, with strong features and smooth skin marred only by several days' growth of facial hair. I fancied I could see something of the wild in him.

About half way through the meal I set my fork aside and took a long drink of beer—it was wonderfully cold and smooth. Instead of retrieving my fork I rolled the frosted bottle between my palms.

"You have questions," Luke said, continuing to eat. How did he know I was biting my lip to keep my curiosity to myself? He made an encouraging gesture with his free hand. "Go on."

I fought it for all of half a second before I gave in to the intense need to know everything I could about him. "You live alone, but I always believed that werewolves lived in packs." He'd also said it had been a long time since he'd had anyone in his corner, but I kept that to myself.

Placing his fork on the side of his plate, Luke took a moment to wipe his mouth on a napkin. "Ideally that's true, but it's not always possible. I lost my pack, my *family*, shortly after the millennium. There was a house fire."

The word *millennium* caught my attention, and I frowned. "It wasn't an accident, was it?"

He shook his head slowly. "The-the doors and windows had been barricaded from the outside before the fire was started. They…" He paused and cleared his throat before continuing. "They couldn't get out."

The raw pain in his eyes tore at my heart. "Tell me about them?"

He seemed surprised by my question, but pleasantly so, if his smile was any indication. "I grew up in Somerset. My parents were apple growers, and had a small cider mill. They'd been mates since they were seventeen and my dad always introduced my mum as his *bride*. I had two younger brothers, twins, Rory and Daniel. They were a couple of absolute tearaways — if there was a way to get into trouble, they would find it." He laughed quietly, shaking his head, then his expression turned soft. "My little sister Lucy, the youngest by several years, was our princess. She had us all wrapped around her little finger the first time she smiled — she had the sweetest temperament of anyone I've ever met. Hang on a sec." He left the room quickly, and I wondered if I'd upset him by making him remember a time that must still be a source of crippling pain.

I considered whether or not I should follow, but before I'd reached a decision he was back, carrying something.

"A family friend took this photo just a few weeks before… She gave it to me when everything else was lost in the fire." He handed me the photograph, framed in rich mahogany.

"You looked very happy together," I said, taking in the smiling faces of the adults, the mischief in the grins of the twin boys, and the absolute innocence of the little girl sitting atop the shoulders of a very youthful looking Luke. My chest hurt to think about what the very near future held for the small group. I handed the picture back to him.

"We were," Luke replied, running his thumb over the glass before setting the picture down on the marble island. "If things had taken a more...natural path, then I would have become the pack Alpha following my father's passing. For a while afterwards, I didn't think I would survive without them."

"I can't even imagine." My mind flashed to my own parents — my dad, the slightly eccentric professor of classics who could speak six languages, and was in line for the job of master of his college, but who would read by candlelight rather than attempt to change a light bulb. And my mum, a former actress turned professional student, currently working on her third degree. I felt sick just thinking about losing them the way Luke's family had been stolen from him. "How *did* you survive, I mean the fire? That is, if you don't mind me asking."

Luke had begun loading up the dishwasher, but stopped and turned back to me. "I was sixteen at the time, out with my friends." He smiled again. "Running a little wild, y'know?"

"When I was sixteen, 'running a little wild' meant pinching some of dad's scotch and drinking until I puked. I've a feeling it means something different for werewolf boys," I joked, feeling the mood in the kitchen lighten a bit.

He started to laugh, but halfway through a yawn seemed to catch him off-guard. "I guess those drugs still have some kick left in them. I think I'll head up to bed. Come on, I'll show you to one of the guest rooms."

I won't deny I would have much preferred to have been shown to his room, but I thanked him and followed him out of the kitchen. As we were heading upstairs a thought occurred to me and I paused.

"Luke? Why didn't you tell the police what you remembered?"

He stopped and looked back over his shoulder. "I didn't like the way Childes spoke to you, it made me angry." As if that was all the explanation required, he continued on up the stairs. I smiled. It was good enough for me.

Chapter Five

The room Luke showed me to was warm and comfortable, with a huge brass bed and a thick cream carpet. There was also an en-suite bathroom, and the second I opened the door I remembered that I'd been needing to go to the loo ages ago. My bladder made itself known very forcefully, so I relieved myself and had a quick wash in the sink rather than the shower I longed for – I didn't want to risk disturbing Luke.

As I dried my face on a small guest towel, I glanced in the mirrored cabinet over the sink and took stock of what I saw there. My hair, very light brown, though not quite blond, was beginning to curl, as it did when it was in need of a cut. I hadn't bothered to shave during my weekend away, so there was a couple of days' worth of scruff on my chin, and my blue eyes looked dull and tired after such a long, dramatic day. I knew, without false modesty, that I was considered to be good looking, and I tried to keep fit, but I'd always been a little on the thin side, nothing like as broad or muscular as Luke. I wondered what he saw when he looked at me?

I turned away and went back into the bedroom, where I stripped down to my boxers and climbed under the thick blue quilt. The bed was as comfortable as it was big, the pillows soft and plentiful, and after the day I'd had I could feel the need for sleep begin to weigh me down. I closed my eyes and felt like I was just dozing off when a sound — the wind in the trees, the creak of a floorboard — brought me back. Blinking, I glanced at the clock on the table by the bed and saw that it was, in fact, after one in the morning. I'd been asleep for over an hour.

Lying still, watching the dance of shadows on the ceiling, I listened until I heard the noise again. Definitely inside the house, but getting farther away. It was probably just Luke getting up for a drink or a pee, maybe both, but I found it difficult to settle back down again. After a few minutes I pushed the covers aside and climbed out of bed. There was a dark towelling robe hanging on the back of the door, I slipped it on and quietly left the room.

The door to Luke's room was lying open, as was that of the bathroom, so I made my way downstairs, and saw a dim light coming from the direction of the living room.

"Luke?" I tapped softly on the door, then opened it and stuck my head into the room.

Luke was sitting on the edge of one of the sofas, hunched over, hands pushing damp hair back from his face. Even in the poor light of a single lamp I could see the darker patches of sweat staining his T-shirt. He was trembling.

Without a second thought I rushed to him, dropped to my knees in front of him. "What is it? What's happened?"

He shook his head and tried to smile. "It's nothing, go back to bed."

"It's obviously not nothing," I said, taking note of his sickly pallor. He was rubbing his fingers together, flexing and un-flexing his hands, much as he had earlier. "Are your hands sore?" God alone knew how long he'd been tied up.

"No, not pain, just…" He paused, frowning. "You know that feeling you get when your foot goes to sleep, the tingles and prickles when the blood starts to flow again?"

"Pins and needles?" I asked.

He nodded. "I have that, but all over. Every inch of me feels like that."

"Is that what woke you?"

The colour started to return to his face, and he smiled a little sheepishly. "No, I had…well, I guess you'd call it a nightmare. My bedroom suddenly felt too dark and claustrophobic."

I wanted to pull him into my arms, the way one would a vulnerable child, but kept my hands to myself. "That's hardly surprising, considering what you've obviously been through. Can I get you anything?"

Smile deepening, he shook his head. "No, thanks. I'll be fine in a minute or two. Why don't you go back to bed?"

I didn't want to leave him there like that, but I couldn't think of any reason to remain. I got to my feet and dug my hands into the pockets of the robe so that I wouldn't give in to the urge to touch him. "Okay, but if you want to just talk, or anything, you know where I am." My feet dragged on the way to the door, but Luke didn't turn or call me back, so I made my way back upstairs.

It was some time before I felt my body relax again, and I only began to doze off when I heard the door to Luke's bedroom close quietly.

* * * *

It was barely seven when I woke the next morning. I groaned and stretched until my toes peeked out from under the quilt. The room was a little cooler, so I guessed that the heating hadn't come on yet. I tucked my feet back under the covers and relished the luxury of my situation for a few more minutes.

But the stubble on my chin started to itch, and when I raised a hand to scratch it, I caught a whiff of yesterday's sweat and grimaced. A shave and shower were in order as soon as possible.

I pushed the covers aside reluctantly and grabbed my clothes from the chair beside the bed. It would be nice to have a change of clothes, too. I was thankful that I had my weekend bag in the car, and shoved my bare feet into my shoes so that I could go down and fetch it.

The house was quiet, with only the ticking from the long-case clock at the end of the hall breaking the silence.

My gaze was drawn to Luke's door, and I bit my lip, wondering how he was feeling after his bad night, and if he'd managed to get any sleep. I thought about knocking on the door, then reconsidered — maybe he was sleeping now? The answer was quickly supplied when the door I'd been staring at swung open. My gut clenched, my groin tightened and heat bloomed in my chest when I caught sight of him.

The low-slung sleep trousers revealing the jut of his hip bones, the broad, well-defined chest, and wide, powerful shoulders—any one of these would have been enough to light the fire kindling in the pit of my stomach. All three combined hit me with the force of a blow, and between one ragged breath and the next, I was rock hard and aching. But when I lifted my gaze to his face I saw there a look of such untamed, savage need, that I was almost robbed of the ability to breathe altogether.

"I've been waiting for you to wake," he said, low and rough. "I woke hours ago, but I've been waiting for you."

My mouth was dry as dust, and I had to swallow a couple of times before I could speak—even then, my voice was barely loud enough to be heard over the thundering of my heart. "Y-you have?"

"I could smell you," he declared, eyes narrowed, and I knew he wasn't talking about yesterday's sweat. He came closer, his movements measured and graceful. "I slept for a while when I went back to bed, but when I woke again…you were all around me, tempting me, *tormenting* me."

The intensity of his regard should have concerned me. There was something almost fierce glittering in his eyes, and he was bearing down on me with determination vibrating through his magnificent body. But instead, I felt drawn to him, pulled in as if I had no say in the matter. I stumbled forward as my brain tried to keep up with the dictates of my body, and he reached out, wrapped his hands around my arms, not to steady me, but to drag me against him.

He leant down then, tucked his face into the curve of my neck, and inhaled deeply. "Oh, my God, you smell incredible," he groaned, then emitted a long, low-pitched *whine*. It sounded…animalistic. I knew in that second what had happened—the tingling and prickling all over his body—the drugs had been banished from his system and his werewolf senses had been restored. A thrill ripped through me. I gasped and let my head fall back when his teeth brushed lightly against my throat.

"*Yes,*" he proclaimed, lifting his head to let me see the shine of triumph in his eyes. "You know, don't you? You know that you're mine. *Mine!*"

Oh, fuck, *yes.* I not only knew, but on some primal level I accepted, *rejoiced,* in it. Everything in me wanted to offer myself up to him in supplication. He wasn't just an Alpha, he was *my* Alpha. It made no sense. I barely knew him. But at the same time, nothing had ever been clearer.

"I thought I was joking, when I talked of Fate throwing me in your path, but when I woke up with your scent in my nostrils and nothing else mattered half so much as being with you, I knew it wasn't a joke." He lifted his hands to cup my head, thumbs brushing my cheekbones. "You understand this, don't you? We were meant to meet, meant to be."

It was inexplicable, but I *did* understand. There was a sense of rightness about being here with this man. I lifted my hands to rest them on his bare chest, and that first touch of skin sent a jolt of pure pleasure right to my bones. His nipples hardened under my palms and I moaned. I wanted to climb inside him and stay there, but it was so much more than lust—though God knows there was no shortage of that. What I was experiencing ran far deeper than physical desire. It was elemental. "*Mine,*" I said, clenching my fingers so that my nails dug into his skin.

His response was a feral grin, and a slight flexing of his shoulder muscles before he dropped his hands, grabbed my arse, and hauled me up against him. Six feet two and I was being lifted off the floor like I weighed nothing—it shouldn't have been such a turn on. He took a couple of steps to the side and hiked me up higher, pressing me back against the wall beside the guest room door and, in an attempt to get him as close as possible, I wound my legs around his waist and hooked my ankles together at the small of his back. It was such a fucking rush, to be with a man who, with no visible effort, could take me like this.

"Not yet," he said, and ground his hips into mine, letting me feel the hard ridge of his cock pushing insistently at the front of his trousers. "But soon."

My head felt a little hazy, and I was having trouble following his words. I stopped trying altogether when he lowered his head again, and this time his mouth caught mine in a kiss so deep and thorough it was like *he* was trying to crawl inside *me*. My lips parted under the press of his tongue. It swept into my mouth, tasting, tangling with my own. I pushed back, curled my tongue around his and sucked until he moaned. God, he tasted good. I twisted my fingers in his hair and held him close, just in case he had any idea about breaking the kiss.

Instead, he pushed me farther back into the wall, until my shoulder blades protested, and he tightened his grip on my arse, fingers contracting and loosening, rolling our pelvises together so that I wanted to scream at how good it felt.

We breathed through our noses, harsh and uneven, but he seemed as reluctant as I was to break even for air. Mouths wide and tongues thrusting, hands clutching, hips circling and straining...it was wonderful, but it wasn't nearly enough.

It was as though he had the ability to read my mind when, before my thought was even completely formed, he tore his mouth from mine and said in a gravelly voice, "Want more. Have to have you."

"Yes!" I cried, need and anticipation sweeping over me like a tidal wave. I ducked my head to nip along his jaw, dropping lower to lick at his throat and suck on his Adam's apple. He tasted like salt and desperation.

Still holding me easily, though I detected a tremble in his limbs that I would have bet had nothing to do with the strain of carrying me, he turned towards his own bedroom. "I want you in *my* bed," he said, though it sounded more like a demand. One I was happy to meet.

He set me on my feet beside a wide, carved mahogany bed, and immediately went to work on my clothes. There was nothing gentle about the way he stripped me, and I'm sure I heard a few seams give under the rough treatment, but it was exactly what I wanted—what I needed. I kicked my shoes off just as my trousers fell to my ankles, and I quickly cast them aside too, even as I tucked my hands into the waistband of Luke's sleep trousers.

For a minute, when I cupped my hands around the heated, rock hard flesh of his arse, I got side-tracked, lost in the feel of him, before I remembered that I wanted him naked, *now*. I pushed at the cotton, but Luke stepped back, just out of my reach.

"Get on the bed," he said. I'd never been into the whole giving orders thing in the bedroom, but a shiver ran down my spine at his words and the timbre of his voice, so I did as he'd said, settling in the middle of the dark blue quilt.

He just looked at me for long seconds, his gaze hot, chest rising and falling on shallow breaths. My own eyes weren't still. They took in every inch of him that I could see, from the top of his rumpled blond head to his narrow waist, and every curve and indent in-between. He was nothing short of majestic. Then he hooked his thumbs into the waistband of his trousers and peeled them away, and I was forced to re-evaluate. Majestic simply didn't cover it. Between his hips, nestled in a thatch of dark gold hair that didn't know the meaning of 'man-scaping', his cock stood up, thick and long, curving towards those impossibly perfect abs.

"Oh, holy fuck," I breathed, and had to swallow when my mouth watered. I wanted to touch him, taste him and ride him until I couldn't see straight, all at once. My fingers twitched and I lifted a hand to him.

He climbed on the bed beside me, and settled himself between my eagerly parted thighs. "You're beautiful," he said, propping himself up on one arm while he lazily explored my body with his other hand. He dragged his calloused fingers over my skin, leaving a trail of fire in their wake, over my chest and my belly, and down to my hip. The back of his hand brushed against the tip of my dick, and I gasped and arched under him, stomach muscles contracting almost painfully at the sharp stab of pleasure. "I couldn't have wished for a more perfect mate."

Mate? That meant...Jesus, what did that mean again? It sounded so much *more* than 'mine'. But my mind was so foggy, I'm sure I wouldn't have recognised my own face in the mirror.

"Forever," Luke said, answering the question I hadn't asked. His voice sounded awed and I felt the backs of my eyes begin to prickle with some unknown, but profound, emotion.

I closed my thighs around his hips and canted them up. "Please, Luke." I'd never experienced need like it. My whole body was begging for him.

"I can't promise to be gentle, but I need you so much, Hal," he said. As he spoke, he reached over to the table by the bed and retrieved a bottle of lube. He dropped it beside my hip, then palmed the back of my left thigh and pushed my leg up and out, so that I was completely open to him.

My hole convulsed in anticipation and a bead of pre-cum dripped from my cock onto my belly. When Luke dipped his head and lapped it up, I released a choked cry and caught the quilt in a death grip. I was lightheaded and hot, and felt like I might suffocate in my own skin.

I thought I might bite through my lip at the first touch of his slick finger against my entrance. I lifted my hips to meet him, pleading, my head moving back and forth on the pillow. *God*, it was too much. I was strung taut and ready to snap at any minute.

His prep was blessedly brief, then he was sinking into me, stretching me. He growled in the back of his throat and his eyes were diamond bright. "Perfect," he exclaimed, pushing in until he was buried to the hilt inside me.

If I'd been able to form rational thought or speech I would have agreed. But my mind and body were consumed by the feel of him. I was full, physically, emotionally. Something niggled at me, but was quickly forgotten when he began to move.

"You were made for me," he groaned, withdrawing almost all the way then pushing in again, his skin flushed and damp. "We fit like we were designed as part of a pair—your sweet, tight hole and my cock."

I lifted my hands to his head and pulled him into a kiss so fierce I tasted blood, whether it was his or mine, I had no idea. My whole body was quivering with the strain on my muscles, and there was so much pressure in my head that I felt sure it must be about to explode. "Yes, oh *fuck* yes." My grip on his hair must have been painful, but if I was hurting him he showed no signs of it.

The snap of his hips became increasingly urgent, almost violent. I let go of his hair and reached down to grab his arse, urging him on, sobbing every time the head of his dick hit my prostate. The movements of our bodies, pressed so closely together, provided all the delicious friction my own cock needed. My back bowed and my breath hitched, and I came so hard that the warm wetness hit my chin and my body jerked like I was in the throes of a seizure.

Luke was still thrusting, his rhythm erratic. His fingers dug into my thigh where it was pushed back against my chest, and perspiration shone on his brow. His hips stuttered and he gasped, then, just as I felt the rush of his seed inside me, he lowered his head and sunk his teeth into the meat of my shoulder, hard enough to hurt, but not with enough force to break the skin. I cried out in shock, not only at the pain, but at the second orgasm it ripped from my exhausted body.

Chapter Six

"I love your freckles," Luke said, tired humour in his voice as he dragged his tongue lazily over my shoulder.

"You bit me," I accused, but I couldn't find it in me to sound in the least annoyed. I actually kind of liked that I'd driven him to such heights of passion. I turned my head on the pillow, all the exertion I had the energy for right then, and watched as he traced the outline of the bite mark with the tip of his tongue, a small V of concentration between his eyebrows. I felt a tingle in my balls, but I wasn't getting it up without a block and tackle for at least another half an hour.

A slow smile turned up his mouth, and he glanced at me from under his lashes. "Just staking my claim."

I shifted slightly and moaned at the pleasurable burn in my arse. "Trust me, I feel thoroughly staked, the bite really wasn't necessary."

Laughter rumbled from his chest and he pinched my arm with the very edge of his teeth. "Afraid you might catch rabies?"

That niggle I'd felt earlier returned with the force of a hammer blow, pulling me off the happy little cloud I'd been floating on. "We didn't use a condom." It would have been pointless to ask myself what I'd been thinking, because there had been no real thought involved. A flicker of panic ignited in my chest, and a silent chorus of *stupid, stupid, stupid,* sounded in my head.

"Hal." His voice seemed to come at me from a distance, but I couldn't quite focus on it. "Hal," he repeated, this time shifting so that he was lying on me, a grave expression on his face. The weight of his long, hard body got my attention as no words could. I blinked up at him, and knew that if I could go back and change things, I wouldn't. It didn't make me feel any less foolish.

"I'm an idiot," I said, giving voice to my thoughts. "I just got carried away."

The return of Luke's smile made me frown in confusion. How could this be anybody's idea of funny?

He brought a hand up and smoothed his fingers over my forehead. "You have nothing to worry about. I'm a werewolf, remember? No human diseases can survive in my body, and there is nothing that I can pass on to you." He trailed his fingers down my cheek and stroked my lips with his thumb.

The relief I felt at his words was acute, immediately unravelling the tension that had coiled in me. But, unbelievably, it was eclipsed by the renewed desire rekindled by his touch. It was like I was in thrall to him.

"Besides," he continued, pressing his thumb briefly between my lips, and gasping when I touched it with the point of my tongue. "You're the first man I've ever been with like that. I've always used condoms before — not because it was necessary, but because I never wanted to be completely bare with anyone but my mate."

There was that *forever* thing again. "So, you were saving yourself for me?" I asked. It was meant to be a joke, but I couldn't quite meet his eyes.

"Tell me what's troubling you," he said quietly, turning us so that we were lying on our sides, face to face. He wrapped his arm around me and moved his hand in soothing circles on my back.

I huffed a laugh and laid a hand on his chest. "Well, for one thing, you seem to have this unnerving ability to see into my head." I smoothed my hand over his skin and noticed for the first time that the cuts and bruises, and the burns from the stun gun, had faded so that they were nothing more than faint red marks.

"You have a very expressive face, my Hal, and right now it's telling me that something is bothering you deeply."

It seemed pointless to dissemble — he'd probably see through any pretence in a heartbeat. So I took a deep breath and forced myself to meet his eyes. "You said forever."

"And this distresses you?" he asked. He never stopped moving his hand on my back.

I considered his question for a moment, then shook my head. "Not distress, as such, but..." I couldn't think with his hands on me, and I'd begun to slide my foot absently up and down his calf, so I moved out of his embrace to sit, cross-legged, just out of his reach. He didn't try to stop me, but lay with his head propped up on his hand, watching, waiting. "You're a werewolf, and when a werewolf meets the person intended to be their mate, they know it immediately, yes?"

"Generally, yes, unless our systems are pumped full of pharmaceuticals, then it takes a little longer." He edged his fingers slowly towards my knee, but stopped just short of touching me.

I curled my fingers into my palm to resist the urge to take his hand. "Well, I'm human, and it *always* takes us longer to come to decisions like that. So, while I feel this...*unimaginable* connection with you, to give that kind of commitment after less than twenty-four hours is just...impossible." I wanted to apologise, but my throat tightened around the words. I could only take my turn watching, waiting for his reaction.

When it came, it was not at all what I expected. Luke's lips parted on a wide smile and he looked almost relieved. "God, but you had me worried there." He sat up and leaned over to wrap one hand around the back of my neck, the other coming to rest on my chest, just over my heart.

I was baffled, and it must have shown, because he laughed lightly and explained, "Every instinct I have tells me that we're bound, Hal, and this fills me with such joy. But I understand your reservations—I would no more ask you to go against your nature than I could deny my own. We're destined, you and I, and I can wait until your human heart is ready to accept it."

It was said with such quiet conviction that it took my breath away. I lifted my hand to his face, traced the contours of his cheekbones, his nose and the dip of that dimple in his cheek. "Will-will you let me see you?"

He seemed puzzled for a second, then his eyes widened in comprehension. "You mean...?"

A mixture of excitement and apprehension swirled in me, and I nodded. He looked pleased at my request and slid off the bed.

A frisson of shock chased through me. "Now? You're going to do it now?" I glanced in the direction of the window, and the weak November sunlight struggling through the clouds.

"I was born a werewolf, Hal," Luke explained. "So while the phases of the moon have some effect on my behaviour, I'm not at the mercy of them—I control when I shift."

Okay, so *now* then. It felt surreally like I was about to watch a live action horror movie.

He looked down at his hands, and I remembered him doing the same thing on that dark road and in the hospital. My attention, however, was dragged forcefully back to the moment when his nails, slightly ragged from his adventures, but still recognisably human, began to grow and sharpen, darkening, thickening. I could only stare, stunned into silence and inaction as his fingers curled and his skin, starting on the backs of his hands, and travelling rapidly along his arms and over his body, seemed to ripple with underlying pressure. Hair, no, *fur*, burst through his flesh, and, to the accompaniment of bones lengthening, muscles stretching and joints popping, Luke dropped onto all fours. It was beyond incredible to watch, and I did so while barely breathing. His jaw bone seemed to almost unhinge and elongate, until what had been a nose and mouth was now a muzzle. It must have hurt—how could such a transformation be anything but intensely painful? But when he threw his head back and howled, honest to God *howled*, far from being a cry of agony, it sounded more like an exclamation of joy.

When the transition was complete, I was looking not at Luke the man, but at a stunningly beautiful beast with a white-blond colouring that made me think of an arctic wolf. His eyes, cool, ice blue, were so startlingly familiar that, had I not just seen him shift from one state to the other, I'm certain I would still have recognised the wolf as Luke. I got slowly to my knees on the bed and inched towards the edge.

"You're not going to bite me again, are you?" I asked, only half joking, as I glanced at the, quite frankly, terrifying mouthful of teeth Luke now possessed.

He moved forwards on paws big enough to take my head off with one casual swipe, and my pulse quickened as I fought my fight or flight instinct and remained still. The bed, possibly an antique or reproduction, sat high off the floor, but the wolf — *Luke* — still had to dip his head to nudge at my hand where it was resting on my knee. His tongue was warm and a little rough when he licked my fingers, and I laughed at the tickle of his breath against my skin.

"I'm going to touch you," I said, moving tentatively. "But I don't want you to be offended, because I'm not, y'know, *petting* you. Okay?"

He nudged me again, more forcefully this time, and, smiling, I took this for permission. I smoothed my hand over his head, and Jesus, even at its full span, my hand was dwarfed by the size of his skull. On the surface the fur was fairly coarse, but as I sank my fingers in deeper, I found that it was thick and soft underneath. He pushed his head into my palm, rubbed it against me and made a soft growling noise in the back of his throat. I intuitively knew the sound to be one of pleasure, and redoubled my efforts, scrubbing my fingers through his fur until his eyes closed.

All misgiving gone, I leaned over and pressed my face to his. Luke responded by tilting his head and licking from my chin to my forehead in one stroke. I laughed my delight. "A kiss from a wolf?" I asked, and dodged him when he clearly made to repeat the action.

Then, without any warning, he turned and rushed out of the bedroom door. I waited for a bit to see if he would return, and when he didn't I jumped off the bed and grabbed my T-shirt and boxers. I stumbled into them as I hurried after him. I followed the thump of his paws on the stairs, then the click of claws on the tile floor, into the kitchen. I arrived just in time to see him disappear through the patio doors.

Concern stabbed at me—what if someone saw him? But I needn't have worried. When I stepped out onto the patio I saw what I believed to be the reason Luke had rented this house in particular. It sat in perhaps three or four acres of land, surrounded by a wall at least eight feet tall, and inside the wall, trees had been planted, lending the property even more privacy.

I shivered in the cold air as I looked around. When I saw him, however, all thought of my own discomfort faded. My heart felt like it was swelling in my chest, and a smile so wide it almost hurt lifted my mouth.

Luke was bounding around the garden, leaping over the patches where there would no doubt be flower beds in summer, weaving in and out of trees and even peeing up against the wall of a small structure at the very bottom of the garden that looked like some kind of guest house. I laughed quietly as I hoped that he had no intention of marking me as his in the same manner—water sport really wasn't one of my kinks.

When he saw me, or perhaps he *smelt* me, he came tearing up to the house with such speed and purpose that my smile faded and I took a step backwards. "Oh, shit." My foot hit the step behind me, but I managed to stay upright. I was absolutely certain that wasn't going to last long. I could only watch, mouth gaping and eyes wide, as he drew closer with alarming speed, and I thought of how he'd launched himself at me when we'd first met. The weight of him then, though enough to send me flying, was surely nothing compared to his altered form. *I'm going to die*, I thought, as he bore down on me. *I'm going to be squashed to death under a mountain of muscle and fur.* When he was within a few feet of me, and still going, I grimaced and considered something I hadn't in years—praying.

He leapt then, and my arms came up in an automatic defensive gesture, but between leaping and landing he changed back into Luke the man, and instead of crashing into me, he grabbed me up, tossed me over his shoulder and swept me into the kitchen. I was flat on my back on the island, gasping for breath, with a grinning Luke leaning over me before I knew what was happening.

"*Fuck*, that felt good," he exclaimed and, reaching for the waistband of my shorts, ripped them off. "But this is going to feel even better."

I grabbed the sides of the island and held on while he pulled me forward, so that my arse was hanging over the edge, his big hands pushing my calves up to rest on his shoulders. He was flushed and energised, and his eyes retained a wild gleam. My body responded instantly, hardening and arching up to meet him.

"You're still slick from earlier," he said, and I silently thanked God for it when he pushed two thick fingers into me without preamble. "And so fucking tight—I wonder what it would take to get my whole fist up there."

I shuddered and white-knuckled the marble. "Jesus, Luke. One way or another, you're going to fucking kill me." I pushed down on his fingers, three now, and sucked in a ragged breath at the pleasure that lanced through me.

"Then we'll go together," he replied, removing his fingers and thrusting into me in one long, powerful movement.

My T-shirt clad shoulders slid against the smooth surface at my back as he pounded into me, over and over again, his grip on my hips almost painful. *We shouldn't be doing this*, a little voice at the back of my head nagged. Luke had been abducted, held captive and tortured. The journalist in me said we should be out there finding out why that had happened to him, bringing the guilty parties to justice. But, Jesus, it felt so fucking *good*. I could do little more than hang on and enjoy the ride, the voice becoming more vague and distant with every touch.

He released one of my hips and brought a trembling hand up to my mouth, index finger tracing my lips before dipping inside. I closed my lips around it, and licked and sucked until he was moaning, his eyes hooded, chest heaving.

"Will you suck my cock so sweetly, my Hal?" he asked, his voice rough. He thrust hard, as if to punctuate his question, and I groaned and bit down on his finger. His eyes glittered and he slid his other hand from my hip, under my rumpled T-shirt, and over my chest. My dick throbbed and pulsed when he took one of my nipples between his fingers and gave it a little twist. "You like that, hmm? What else do you like, I wonder? Would you like *my* mouth on *your* cock? Or my tongue in your arse?"

Holy *fuck*. "Yes, yes and, oh *fuck* yes!" I let go of one side of the island and wrapped my hand around my dick, giving it a quick squeeze so that I wouldn't come too soon. The feel of him inside me was just too damn good to be rushed.

He laughed, and it was deliciously dirty. "Don't hold back, bring yourself off for me."

"Not yet," I breathed, circling my hips against his. "A little longer, just a…little…longer." But I could already feel that tell-tale tingle at the base of my spine, and my balls were pulled up tight against my body.

"We have all the time in the world, my Hal, don't deny yourself." Luke pulled his hand out from under my T-shirt and wrapped it around mine on my cock. With slow strokes perfectly timed to his thrusts, he brought me to a shivering, panting release. He tumbled into the abyss soon after me, muttering whisper-soft endearments of *beautiful*, *wonderful* and *mine*.

Chapter Seven

"I love your curls," Luke said, nuzzling into the back of my neck where my hair was curling damply from the shower. He had his arms wrapped around me, hands resting on top of the thick blue towel secured at my waist.

I grinned at our reflection in the mirror over the sink—we looked damn good together. "More than my freckles?" I asked, sweeping the razor over my chin one last time, before rinsing it in the basin and wiping the remaining foam from my face.

"Hmm, difficult question. It might require further, and extensive, investigation." He turned his head to press a line of kisses along my shoulder, and the tips of his fingers dipped under the towel.

Laughing, even as a thrill of desire nudged at me, I slapped his hand away. "Come on, you need to shave. While I love the wild man look on you, my skin is starting to shred."

"But I don't wanna," he whined, hands sweeping over my chest while his tongue went to work on the whorl of my ear. "I wanna play."

I shivered and my cock stirred, but I resisted. "Sorry, lover, but my arse is off-limits for at least the next few hours. You didn't warn me about the recovery time of werewolves." I turned to face him, then steered him around so that his back was to the counter beside the sink, and gestured for him to hop up. I moved to stand between his knees, tucked his damp hair behind his ears then reached for the shaving foam.

"But you have such a fine arse," he said, reaching around me to grab two handfuls of it. When his fingers began a slow massage I moaned and pressed my dick against the front of the counter. I'd never been this on edge in my entire adult life. One touch from Luke, one glance, and I was hard and ready to go again. He was like some kind of organic Viagra.

My hands trembled as I smoothed the shaving foam onto his jaw and cheeks. "I'm about to hold a razor to your throat, you might want to stop that, just in case."

He grinned, unconcerned. "Do I get you all hot and bothered, my Hal?"

"Behave," I said, pinching his cheek, but there was no heat in the demand, only in my blood. I forced myself to concentrate and began to draw the razor over his skin. His hands remained on my backside, but at least he'd stopped squeezing. I could feel his eyes on my face, and a soft smile played around the corners of his mouth.

"I think I like having you service me like this," he said huskily, when I withdrew to rinse the razor. "I never knew that shaving could be such a sensual experience."

Just breathing near this man was becoming a sensual experience for me. I shaved his top lip last, then slid my thumb over the little dip under his nose, and dropped the razor into the sink. "Are you telling me that you'll be wanking off to the memory of me shaving you?"

His laughter was thunderous and joyful, and he pulled me into a hug. Maybe it was the sex, or maybe it was just that he was *himself* again, but he showed no signs of lingering distress from his nightmare. "I sincerely hope there won't be much call for such a solitary act, now that I have you in my life."

He smelt like soap and shampoo, with an underlying hint of musk. I hooked my fingers over the towel at his waist and buried my face in his neck, inhaling his scent and tasting him with little flicks of my tongue that made him shudder. I could feel the urgent press of his erection against my stomach, and drew back, smiling. I parted his towel and let it fall to the sides, then settled my gaze on his rigid shaft, standing straight out from his body as if trying to get my attention. "My, my, Mr Wolf, what a big dick you have."

Laughter once more spilled from his lips, but it turned into a choked off groan when I lowered my head and took him deep into my mouth.

* * * *

The intercom by the kitchen door buzzed when we were drinking coffee after a late breakfast. Luke pushed away from the table overlooking the garden and crossed to answer it. I took the opportunity to admire the way his bum looked in the washed out jeans he was wearing, and the way his shoulders filled out his shirt.

"Delivery for Mr Tallis from Albright Art Supplies," said the slightly crackly, disembodied voice.

Luke's eyes lit up and he pushed the button to open the gates. "Back in a minute," he called over his shoulder as he headed out of the kitchen. I settled back in my chair to finish my coffee while I waited, letting my gaze drift over the frosty scene beyond the windows, and smiling when I thought of Luke cutting loose out there. My soft laugh blew a curl of steam across the surface of my coffee. There was nothing even remotely funny about what had happened to Luke, of course, but I couldn't help finding some amusement in spending almost an hour watching him, a *supernatural being*, do all the mundane little things like reporting his driving licence missing, cancelling his credit cards and tracking down his 'missing' car to the garage where he'd left it.

When he returned, Luke was carrying a large cardboard box and sporting a broad smile. "Would you like to see my work?" he asked.

Interest roused, I set my cup aside and nodded. "Yes, is it in there?"

He tucked the box under one arm and held the other out to me. "Come with me."

"Okay then." I got to my feet, took his hand, and allowed myself to be led out of the house, into the garden and towards the smaller building at the bottom. Dressed as I was, in just a white V-neck T-shirt and jeans, I was chilled by the time we got there. I rubbed at the goose bumps on my arms as he opened the door, and hurried quickly inside.

The building was bigger than it seemed on the outside. It was clearly an artist's studio, dominated by a long, wide work table that ran nearly the length of the back wall, half of the table taken up by what looked like some kind of light box. Bottles, jars and boxes filled the shelves that lined the wall opposite, and all manner of tools, some of them quite lethal looking, hung from hooks and filled clay pots. My attention was captured almost immediately by the display at the farthest end of the studio.

Hanging from thin wires attached to the ceiling were a dozen stained glass panels, each depicting a different scene of children at play — one had two girls playing hopscotch, another a group of boys battling it out with marbles, and still others included children playing with hula-hoops, playing 'Ring of Roses' and skipping rope. They were stunning, and the way the light from the windows behind seemed to illuminate the panels, throwing their colours over the surrounding area, was simply breathtaking. I lifted a hand, but didn't touch. Instead I turned to Luke, and I was surprised to see a look of uncertainty on his face.

"You did these?" I asked, and he nodded. I had to look at them again, so I turned back. There was such happiness in the images that I couldn't stop the smile I felt breaking out. "They're... Oh, my God, Luke, they're *incredible*."

He came up beside me, set his parcel down on the table and draped an arm loosely around my waist. "I'm glad you like them. They're a special commission for a children's toy museum being built in Manchester. I just have another two to complete before I ship them." He indicated the sketches pinned to the wall over the table. One portrayed a spirited game of skittles, and the other was a couple of boys playing with a train set.

"I'm...speechless. Before I met you, I don't remember the last time that happened." Laughter bubbled up in my throat and I turned to face him. His gratification at my words was written large across his face. I took his hands in mine and looked at them like I was seeing them for the first time. I recalled with vivid clarity how the calluses on his fingers felt heavenly against my skin, but now I knew they had been earned in the creation of something exquisite. "Your work is magnificent, Luke. *You're* magnificent."

He withdrew one of his hands from mine and lifted it to spear his fingers through my hair. "I make pretty things, but you, my Hal, you change the world with your words."

Shock widened my eyes. "You know what I do, who I am?"

He smiled and ran a finger around the curve of my ear. "The name Hal *Paxton* rang a bell when Childes said it at the hospital, but it was only at about three this morning, when I was pacing my room waiting for you to wake, that I remembered. Your book is wonderful."

I felt myself blushing with pleasure. "Well, people seem to like it, but as for changing the world, I doubt it."

"I believe the men freed from prison because of you would disagree."

Turning in his arms, I leant back against him and tugged his arms around my waist. In that moment I felt truly blessed, like God himself had smiled down on me. But there was a shadow lurking just beyond the joy I felt. "Luke, would you do something for me?"

"Anything," he replied, without hesitation, resting his chin on the crown of my head.

I smoothed my hands over his and took a deep breath. "Will you...will you go to the police, report what happened to you?"

Behind me, his body stiffened, but he didn't move away. "I have nothing to tell them, Hal. I don't remember anything more than I told you, and that's hardly enough to build a case on."

I twisted in his arms so that I could see his face. The shadow was there, in his eyes. "You may not be able to give them much information, but they can still investigate. Don't you want...don't you *need* to know what happened to you?" I found that I did, and it wasn't all professional curiosity.

Resistance tightened his jaw, but there was resignation there too, and, after a few seconds of silent consideration, he nodded. "I won't deny that it's been on my mind. I'm safe now, healed, but what if I wasn't the only one? What if there are others who didn't get away? Yes, I'll talk to the police. I need to go in to London to collect my car, I'll report it then, since that's where I believe I was...taken."

I smiled and pressed a kiss to his lips. "I never believed in Fate before I met you, but if you think she threw us together on that road in Surrey, then I have a lot to thank her for."

"Why don't you thank me and I'll pass the message on?" he asked, backing me up against the work table, smiling mischievously.

* * * *

We arrived in London at just after two in the afternoon, and I followed Luke's directions to the garage, near Highbury. The mechanic accepted his excuse of a family emergency for not collecting the car sooner, and handed over the keys. Luke drove the car, a grey Toyota Land Cruiser, out onto the street and parked it beside mine, then got out to stand in front of me.

"The café I went to is just along the road there," he said. "And Albrights is around the corner—it's my favourite supplier, and the reason I chose this garage is simply its proximity to the shop. I don't come in to the city often, and when I do, I like to get things done as quickly as possible. It's better to keep a low profile when you're a werewolf."

"What's the last thing you remember about…that day?" I asked.

Though he was looking at me, his eyes became slightly unfocused, and I could tell that he was seeing something else. When he spoke it was slow and considered. "Well, I had coffee and something to eat—roast beef and mustard on wheat bread. Then I went to Albrights, where I spent about…an hour or so. They didn't have the flux brushes I was looking for, so I asked them to have everything delivered when they came in. I headed back towards the garage, took a shortcut through a lane…" His hand jerked up to rest on his chest and he sucked in a sharp breath.

"Luke?" I laid my hand on his arm and gave it a little squeeze. "What is it?"

He shook his head, frowning. "There was a flash, pain in my chest, and I couldn't stay on my feet. I fell to my knees, then…something sharp…" He rubbed at the side of his neck.

"The stun gun and a needle full of drugs," I guessed, swallowing down the bile that rose in my throat.

"When I opened my eyes again it was dark, and after that everything seems…out of my reach, you understand?" The corners of his eyes were tight with strain, and there was a deep V between his eyebrows.

I wanted nothing more than to wrap my arms around him, but I wasn't sure how he felt about public displays of affection, so I pushed my concern down until it was an uncomfortable weight in my stomach. "We should go to the nearest police station, I think, since whatever happened, happened in this area."

Luke's reluctance was clear in his expression, but he nodded. "I'll ask for directions in the garage." He turned to head in that direction, but got no more than a few steps along the pavement when a silver four-wheel drive pulled up in front of the garage, and two men got out.

There was nothing remarkable about them—both were of average height, average build and so very *ordinary* looking. But one look at them and I felt instantly on edge. I pushed away from my car, heart beating faster, and opened my mouth to call out to Luke. But before I got a chance, one of the men pulled what looked like a gun from the inside of his coat, and pointed it at Luke. My heart stopped dead, and the warning froze on my lips, unheard, when the trigger was pulled.

It was a surreal moment, like something from a movie. There was a loud, cracking sound, and Luke was thrown backwards to land almost at my feet. The sight of him, there on the ground, his body jerking like he was having a seizure, and gasping for breath, enraged me. Without thought, I charged towards Luke's attackers. I launched myself at the one with the stun gun and barrelled him to the ground. While he was dazed, the breath knocked from him, I pulled my arm back, then drove it forwards again, meeting his chin with a satisfying crunch.

I had no time to enjoy the moment, however, because the other man landed a kick to my ribs that dislodged me from his associate. I clutched at my side, adrenaline too high at that point to feel any pain, and rolled away, out of reach of his next blow. When his foot found only air this time, it left him a little off balance. I grabbed for it, wrapping my hand around his ankle and giving his leg a good hard yank. He fell backwards, arms wind-milling, and hit the ground with an *oof* of expelled breath.

Dragging in air, I scrambled to my feet and rushed back to Luke. He was still twitching as the electricity jolted through his muscles, but he was already beginning to settle. My heart, however, was not, it was still racing like a train out of control. I wrapped the sleeve of my jacket around my hand, grabbed the insulated wires and ripped the electrodes from Luke's clothing.

The rush of blood in my ears was almost enough to drown out the sounds of cars screeching to a halt, doors slamming and hurried footsteps. I turned in a crouch, ready to fight again, but as I watched, the two assailants were hauled up off the ground by another two men, who quickly handcuffed them. A third man and a woman came towards Luke and me, holding out warrant cards.

"It's okay, Mr Paxton, we're the police," the man said. He dropped to one knee beside Luke, glanced at him with a frown, then turned to the woman. "He's coming round, no need for an ambulance, I think."

I sat back on my heels, more than a little bewildered. "What... I don't..."

The officer smiled at me. "Come on, help me get Mr Tallis to his feet?"

Nodding, I wrapped my hand around Luke's arm and eased my hand under his back. The cop did the same on the other side, and between us we had Luke sitting up, blinking and looking as confused as I felt.

Chapter Eight

"What the hell is going on here?" I demanded of the police officer, resting a hand at the small of Luke's back. He was standing now, and quickly shaking off the effects of the stun gun. With the adrenaline fading from my own system, I was starting to feel the throb in my side, but nothing felt broken or cracked. I'd probably have a nice bruise to go with the one circling my throat.

"I'm sure you have all manner of questions, Mr Paxton," the man replied.

"Yes, not least of which is how exactly you know our names." And why he was smiling—I hadn't had a cop treat me with anything but overt contempt for longer than I could remember.

He nodded. "I promise I'll answer all your questions, if you would accompany us to our office?"

"Luke?" I asked, prepared to take my lead from him.

His eyes were narrowed as he watched the two men who'd attacked us be led away and shoved into the back of a car. "Can I have five minutes alone with them?"

Laughter erupted from the cop in front of us. "I truly wish I could say yes, but, unfortunately…" He shrugged.

I caught a flash of teeth from Luke, and lust stabbed at me. I sensed this was going to be a *thing*. Luke's head snapped around, his attention instantly on me, nostrils flared and pupils blown wide. For a second I thought he was going to go at me right there and then. I was stunned to realise that I wouldn't have put up much of a fight, if any.

"Well, if you gentlemen will just excuse me for a moment?"

I was only peripherally aware of the cop walking away, taking his female colleague with him.

"Luke?" I asked, my hand still at the small of his back clenching in the material of his wool jacket.

"You smell incredible," he ground out. "And when you took on those men, to protect me… I want you so fucking much right now."

Ordinarily, I would have been embarrassed by the little whine I emitted then, but every cell in my body was completely focused on him. I leaned into him, breathed in *his* scent, and shivered at the desire that tingled along my nerves. "God, *yes.*"

He lifted a hand to my face and dipped his head closer. My lips parted in anticipation, eyes dropping to his mouth.

But the kiss I was expecting, aching for, never came. A cough beside us broke the delicious tension of the moment, and we turned our heads in unison to find the cop smiling somewhat sheepishly.

"If it's agreeable to you, I'll drive you both in to the office, and we'll arrange to have your own vehicles brought on?"

What I *wanted* was to tumble into the back of that Land Cruiser with Luke and ride him until he howled.

"Hold that thought," Luke whispered in my ear. He might as well have grabbed my crotch.

I glared at him with all the force I could manage with my brains in my shorts. "One of these days, you're going to tell me how the hell you do that."

Grinning, clearly unrepentant, Luke nudged me forwards. "Come on, dear, let's go with the nice policeman."

While adjusting my trousers as discreetly as possible, I vowed to get even with the rotten tease.

* * * *

The 'nice policeman' was, in fact, Detective Chief Inspector Ken Trask, and his female associate was Detective Inspector Georgie Fisher. They drove us to an old building on the Victoria Embankment, and ushered us up to the fifth floor in a lift that might have been new in the 1920s. I wouldn't have been in the least surprised if the thing was manually operated. The hallway we walked along was lined with small-paned, arched windows and chunky, antique radiators, and pipes ran overhead.

The vintage theme ended abruptly when Trask pushed through the swing doors at the end of the hall, and we stepped into a room that looked like a movie set. The desks were dark wood and acrylic, the chairs those ergonomically designed monstrosities that cut off the circulation to the users' legs after ten minutes. State of the art computers sat on the desks, and the back wall was hung with six large screens operated from a high-tech table in front of them.

"What is this place?" I asked, glancing around warily at the recessed lighting, the shiny hardwood floor, wood-panelled walls and professional grade coffee machine in the corner. No police station I'd ever been in had this kind of budget. There were perhaps a dozen other officers present, each tending to their own tasks and paying us only cursory attention.

"We're a specialised unit—we deal with…high priority crimes," Trask said, leading the way to a room with frosted glass walls and a long, rosewood conference table. "Please, have a seat."

Luke and I sat side by side in chairs upholstered in suede. Trask sat at the head of the table with Fisher to his left, the light from the window behind him falling in a striped pattern through wooden Venetian blinds.

"How can we be of any interest to you?" Luke asked. "While I take my safety and that of my mate very seriously, I hardly think it to be of high enough priority to get your attention."

I flushed at his easy use of the word 'mate', but also felt a flicker of pride.

Inspector Fisher pushed a computer tablet across the table to her boss at his barely noticeable nod.

"I'm about to reveal some information to you, gentlemen. But before I do, I must have your word that it will go no further than this office." Trask arched his eyebrow in our direction, but I couldn't help feeling that he was speaking to me in particular.

I bristled and clasped my hands on the table top. "Does this information have to do with what happened to Luke?"

"I believe so." Trask nodded.

"Then you can be quite assured of my discretion, Inspector." I was certain I hadn't said anything even slightly amusing, but Trask's lips twitched as if he was having trouble keeping his smile from showing. Annoyance pricked at me.

"Mr Paxton—may I call you Hal?" Without waiting for my reply, Trask continued, "Perhaps I should...clear the air before we continue, Hal. Yes, I read your book, and yes, I was disgusted, but not by you. There's no place in today's police service for people like John Stoke and his like—they make the job harder for all of us, and God knows it's not easy to begin with. Unfortunately, there still exists a culture within the service of closing ranks, a kind of loyalty that can be laudable, but is sometimes misplaced. So, while I appreciate that you must be suffering something of a backlash to the publication of your book, I can assure you that you won't find that kind of nonsense here, understood?"

I was a little taken aback, not only at his frank words, but also the tone of sincerity in his voice. I felt the ire leave me, replaced by gratitude. I smiled and nodded. "Understood, Chief Inspector, and appreciated."

"Good, good." He turned back to the tablet, and began tapping at the screen, his expression now very serious. He took a pair of glasses from his inside pocket and perched them on the end of his nose, then dragged a hand through thick, greying hair. I guessed his age to be somewhere in his late forties or early fifties. He was good-looking in a world-weary, bookish way.

"You've been having trouble?" Luke asked, laying one of his big hands over mine. "Why didn't you tell me?"

"It's nothing to worry about, really. I'll tell you later?"

He hesitated before lifting his hand and brushing his thumb once over my cheekbone. I warmed at the touch and the intent behind it. So, now I knew his feelings on PDAs.

Trask cleared his throat pointedly, and we turned our attention back to him.

"In the last six months, four young men have been found, apparently beaten to death, at various points along the coast," Trask began. "These men had several things in common — they all lived solitary lives, no family, very few friends. Forensic testing of their hair showed that they'd been subjected to the same cocktail of drugs as Luke until about a week before they died, and they were all werewolves."

Realisation began to dawn, and I felt quite sick. "You think someone is targeting werewolves? A killer?" Unconsciously I removed my hands from the table and dropped one onto Luke's thigh. His hand covered mine again, and squeezed gently.

"We had believed that this might be the work of a serial killer," Inspector Fisher spoke for the first time. She was a pretty woman who looked remarkably young to carry such a high rank, and the way she wore her blonde hair scraped back in a severe bun did nothing to conceal her relative youth, as I suspected was the aim of such an unattractive style. Her blue eyes, however, were sharp and intelligent. "Deliberately targeting packless wolves."

Luke snarled softly. I leaned closer to him, smoothed my hand along his suddenly tense thigh in an attempt to calm him, even as my own pulse kicked up a notch at the implication of Fisher's words.

"Had believed? Past tense?" I asked.

Trask nodded. He removed his glasses and rubbed his nose before replacing them. "That was our working theory. But what happened today doesn't support that."

"The thugs at the garage?" I guessed. "Serial killers tend to work alone."

"Exactly," Trask confirmed. "For six months we've been investigating the deaths of these young men, with virtually nothing to go on."

"Until now," Fisher added. "If we're right, then Luke is the first survivor of this...whatever the hell this is."

"But how did you find out about me?" Luke asked. "I haven't spoken to the police yet. We were planning on making a report today."

"Childes, the detective who came to the hospital, logged the details of the visit, and marked it for 'No further action'," Trask explained. "Our system here is set up to flag any crimes reported that match certain criteria. Childes' report set off all kinds of alarm bells."

Something unpleasant began to unfurl in my gut as I listened to them speak. Heat spread through me, filled my chest and fired the blood rushing to my head. I wasn't even aware that I was digging my fingers into Luke's thigh until he took my hand in both of his.

"Hal, what's wrong?"

Even the concern in his voice, and the soft way he was smoothing his fingers over mine, failed to quiet the roar of indignation I could feel rising in me. My head felt light as I got to my feet, fury churning in my chest. "You bastards. You unbelievable *bastards*." My voice was surprisingly quiet, considering just how outraged I was.

Luke was standing beside me in an instant, placing himself between me and Trask. He was clearly at a loss. I glanced up at him, at his beautiful face, his gentle eyes, and my anger amped up further still.

"You used him as *bait*," I accused, turning back to Trask. "You've been following him, watching, waiting for someone to try to *hurt him*." I was shaking, and my hands clenched into fists. I'd never had a stronger urge to hit someone in my life.

"Hal, I promise you, there was never any real danger to Luke," Trask reasoned.

"They used a fucking *stun gun* on him," I retorted, shouting now. "What if it had been a real gun? What if they'd *shot* him?" My vision was beginning to grey out at the edges, and I felt like I might throw up, or pass out.

"Ssh, Hal. Calm yourself," Luke said, in a hushed tone. He had his hands on my upper arms and was lowering me back into my chair. When I was seated once more, he crouched beside me and slid his hands up to cup my cheeks.

"You could have been..." And, dear God, my voice broke and I couldn't finish my sentence. But just the thought of it left me feeling bereft.

"Look at me, Hal," he coaxed, and when I did, he smiled — it was a smile meant for me alone. "I'm here, and I'm fine. How could I not be, with you on my side?"

"Georgie, perhaps you could organise some tea?" Trask asked, and out of the corner of my eye I saw Fisher nod and leave the room.

Luke continued to caress my cheeks with his thumbs, and leaned in to rest his forehead against mine. When he spoke again it was too quiet for anyone but me to hear. "I believe your heart has begun to accept our bond, my Hal."

I closed my eyes and breathed deeply in an attempt to get my riotous emotions under control. I didn't offer my agreement, but nor could I find it in me to disagree.

* * * *

"I don't know how much help I will be," Luke said, brow wrinkled with frustration. "I truly don't remember any more than I've already told you." He was standing at the conference room window, his back to the room.

Tea had been served and drunk, and I was feeling considerably less murderous — though, oddly, not at all chagrined by my recent outburst.

"We can do something called a cognitive interview," Fisher explained, tapping her pen against her finger. "We've had a lot of success bringing out deeply buried memories."

Luke turned round and glanced at me. "Have you heard of this?"

"It's an accepted technique," I assured him. "Nothing invasive, nothing that can hurt you."

"Absolutely not," Trask threw in quickly, gaze flicking between Luke and me.

"Okay then." Luke nodded. "Here?"

"These interviews are usually performed one on one," Trask explained. "It helps if there's as little distraction as possible."

"Why don't you come with me, Luke?" Inspector Fisher asked, getting to her feet and gesturing towards the door. "We have a couple of private interview rooms."

I felt strangely reluctant to have Luke out of my sight, but I said nothing as he left with Fisher. The sound of traffic from the road below was all that broke the silence of the room for a few, long minutes.

"So, you're bonded?" Trask asked, finally.

I turned my attention away from the door, and stopped the nervous tap of my fingers on the table top. "We're not... Well, Luke says, but I don't..." I shrugged. "It's complicated.

Trask smiled knowingly. I still kind of wanted to punch him for using Luke that way, but I also found myself liking the man. "You might want to consider listening to him. But, yes, It can be difficult for us humans," he said.

It took a second or two to process his words, and when I realised what he was saying my eyes widened in shock. "You...?"

He huffed a laugh. "My wife is a wolf shifter. We met at university. She came up to me in the library one day, sniffed my neck and told me I was hers."

"What did you do?" I asked, leaning forwards.

"I thought it was all nonsense, of course, but when you're twenty and a strong, beautiful woman wants to claim you..." He grinned.

"You let yourself be claimed," I finished with a laugh.

His smile was pure self-satisfaction. "Over and over again."

Memory tripped down my spine like a caress, and I had to suppress a moan. "How, uh, how did you know? I mean, when did you...accept?"

"Orla — my wife — had a part-time job as a barmaid when we were at uni. One night a customer got a little over friendly and had to be thrown out." Trask scowled as he spoke. "He waited for her and tried to assault her. She was more than capable of taking care of herself, but I felt such blinding rage. I'm normally quite a placid kind of man, but I wanted to tear the bastard limb from limb for even thinking about hurting her. But, it's not something that you accept on an intellectual level, it's more…"

"Instinctual," I supplied. He was describing my own reaction to the attack outside the garage, and again later, in that very room. My eyes went once more to the door of the conference room, and my fingers began tapping again. He just nodded with a small smile.

"We can go and watch, if you like?" he asked. "There's an observation room next door, so we won't interrupt the interview."

I was on my feet before he finished speaking.

The interview room had two armchairs in it. I guessed this wasn't the place they interrogated hardened criminals. Luke was sitting in the one facing the one-way glass between the interview room and the observation room. Fisher was sitting in the other, her back to us.

Luke had his eyes closed, and his hands were gripping the arms of the chair.

"You said you were cold when you woke up," Fisher said. "What kind of floor are you lying on?"

He tilted his head to the side and wrinkled his nose in concentration. "It's…it's cold and hard—stone, I think, not concrete. There's…rope around my wrists. It's tight, rubbing…" He crossed his arms at the wrists to demonstrate.

"Can you smell anything?"

"Stale, the air is stale. There are small windows, up high, but they've been boarded up. But I can smell the earth too, like home…my family home…but *not*." He shook his head, as if he was trying to dislodge a memory.

"You grew up in the country, didn't you, Luke?" Fisher asked. Her voice was soft and rhythmic, almost hypnotic.

"Yes, the country." Luke nodded. "It smelt like the country. Like a farm."

"Can you hear any animals?"

He thought for a second, then shook his head. "No, no animals, just people."

"How many people, Luke?"

"I don't know, a few, maybe. I can hear them talking, laughing...crying."

Fisher leant forwards then, her posture alert. "You can hear crying, Luke? Who's crying?"

"He's close, but not in the same room." Luke's brow furrowed. "He sounds young."

"Is it a child?"

He shook his head. "No, not a child, older...but still young. He's-he's stopped crying—I think they took him away. I can't hear him anymore." This seemed to upset him more than anything else, and my fingers gripped the frame at the bottom of the window.

"Can you tell me about the other people?" she asked, as if trying to distract him.

"Men, they sound like men...heavy footsteps. They're coming again. I-I don't like it when they come. Everything gets hazy...so tired. I can't shift." His chest started to rise and fall, revealing his agitation, and I had to fight the need to go in there and hold him. "Not again. Not this time. There's only one this time."

"How do you get out, Luke?" Fisher asked. She was rapidly scribbling in a notebook, but didn't seem to move her gaze from Luke.

He shook his head. "I don't..."

"Okay, but you see the man coming in? On his own?"

"Yes, he has another needle. Not again. I don't like that." He was rubbing at his neck, the movements jerky and distressed.

"Does he get the needle into you?" she asked.

Luke opened his mouth to speak, but paused. His eyes moved rapidly behind his lids, and a smile tugged at his mouth. "Not this time. I pretend to be asleep. He comes closer and I launch myself at him."

I couldn't help laughing. "Yes, he's good at that."

"He hits the ground," Luke continued. "I grab the needle from him and stick it in his arm. The door's open. There are three other rooms—no, four. But no one else is around down here."

"Down? What makes you say *down here*, Luke?"

"The stairs—there's only one set and they go up. I-I think it's the basement of a house." His smile faded. "I'm looking around, but I can't find the boy. I try to concentrate... My senses are dull, but if I try really hard... I smell humans, but older, no one young. Where is the boy? What have they done to him? Where have they taken him?" He was starting to become quite agitated.

"It's okay, Luke, just concentrate on breathing. Slow, deep breaths." Fisher's voice was gentle, coaxing, but rather than settling down, Luke was becoming increasingly restive.

As I watched, his nails began to transform into sharp, curled claws that threatened to rent gouges in the arms of the chair. Soft undulations disturbed the skin on the back of his hands, and when he sucked in a ragged breath I caught a glimpse of the razor sharp point of a fang.

"I need to go in there," I said, pushing away from the observation glass.

"Georgie knows what she's doing," Ken argued, following me as I crossed to the door.

I lengthened my stride when a low growl reached my ears, and yanked open the door dividing the rooms to find Luke on his feet, arms out at his sides as the shifting musculature of his body strained against the material of his clothing. My knowledge of werewolf lore was pretty much limited to what I'd learnt on those marches during my student days, but I suspected that an Alpha the size of Luke, shifting in anger or distress could not be a good thing.

His attention snapped to me the second I stepped into the room, and his cool blue eyes locked on mine. I moved slowly towards him, hands out in supplication. "You okay, love?"

Georgie came to me and laid a hand on my arm. "It's alright, Hal..." But she got no further.

Behind me Ken yelled, "No, Georgie, don't touch him!" But it was too late. Her hand was on me, and it quickly became very apparent that Luke did not like that at all.

With a roar of fury, Luke bounded across the room, pulled me into his arms and out of Georgie's reach, turned on the petite woman and snarled, "*Mine.*" Wrapped around me as he was, I could feel the thrum of feral rage coursing through his body, the rapid beat of his heart, and the heat of his breath on my neck.

Georgie's eyes were wide with terror as Ken, moving slowly, took hold of her upper arms and backed them out of the room.

"She touched you," Luke growled when the door closed quietly, leaving us alone. His arms tightened around me until I was pressed fully against his hard body. "No one touches you but me."

Common sense told me that fear was the correct emotion for the situation, or, at the very least, irritation at having been so publicly claimed. What I felt, however, was privileged. That someone like Luke, with all his strength and beauty, should want me so fiercely was thrilling and empowering.

I managed to turn in the tight band of his arms, and raised my hands to his face. His eyes flashed, fever bright, and his fangs glistened in the muted, ambient light.

"Only you," I agreed, smoothing my fingers over his cheeks until his eyelids began to droop and his sharp teeth started to recede. "No one but you."

One big hand came up to curl around the back of my head, and claws lightly scraped my scalp when Luke clutched a handful of my hair and tilted my head to the side. He lowered his own head to my neck then, and breathed me in. Against my chest I felt his heartbeat slow down and the tension drain from his body.

"*My* Hal," he sighed, dropping small, damp kisses onto my neck and throat.

Still stroking his cheeks, I manoeuvred him back to his chair, and crouched in front of him. "Why don't we finish this interview up together, just you and me?" I asked, and he nodded, smiling.

For long minutes we did nothing but breathe together, hands never leaving each other's bodies, and a sense of total calm descended on the room.

"Tell me about the rest of the basement," I coaxed.

"All the other rooms are empty," he finally continued. "One room is lighter than the others."

"Where is the light coming from, Luke?"

There was another pause while he thought about it. "The window…there's no board, and the window is broken. I use it to cut the ropes." He took a deep breath. "I can smell fresh air."

"Is that how you get out?"

He nodded. "I cut my feet on the glass, but I'm out…running. It's cold, but I keep running."

"How long do you run for, Luke?"

"I don't know." He shook his head firmly. "I run until I get to the road, but it's still light, so I find somewhere to hide until it gets dark… I-I'm tired again…can't stay awake. The bees… God, they're so *loud*."

Chapter Nine

"Luke, I'm not doubting you, I'm just saying, there are no bees in winter in this country—certainly not enough to qualify as a swarm." Trask sat on the window ledge of the conference room, twirling a pen absently between his fingers.

"And I'm just saying..." Luke scrubbed a hand over his face and pushed away from the conference table. "Never mind. Rationally I know you're right, but damn it, I know what I heard."

"Try to think again, do you remember seeing either of the men who attacked you at the garage before today?" Fisher asked. She was sitting as far from Luke as the room would allow, but was speaking directly to him, as if to prove that her fear had been brief and was now under control. Luke quickly shook his head in answer to her question.

"No. Maybe... *Fuck*, I don't know." He sounded weary, and I could certainly understand why. We'd been in that room for nearly three hours since the end of Luke's interview. *I* was tired and I wasn't the one who was being grilled, although, I had to admit, they were being very civilised about it.

"Could we take a break for a little while, Chief Inspector?" I asked. "I think perhaps we could all use some food and fresh coffee."

Trask nodded and stood. "Yes, of course. I'll arrange to have some food brought in. Any preferences?"

Luke narrowed his eyes. "Steak, *bloody*, no salad."

"As you wish," Trask replied, obviously biting back a smile. "Georgie, why don't we give our guests a moment alone?"

"You're going to have to do better than that, if you want to intimidate him." I smiled, getting up to stand in front of Luke, blocking the path he'd been pacing.

He cocked an eyebrow. "Oh, really? How much better?"

Stepping nearer, I rested a hand on his chest, finally giving in to the need to touch that had been plaguing me for hours. "He's married to a wolf shifter. A female Alpha, from what I gather."

He grinned and perched on the edge of the table, pulling me to stand between his spread legs. "Ah, a *lot* better then." One hand settled on my hip and the other came up to curl around the back of my neck again. I put up no resistance when he urged me closer and brought our mouths together.

After hours of wanting and repressing, the kiss was nothing short of a mutual assault. I speared my fingers through his hair to hold his head and pressed my tongue into his mouth. His lips parted eagerly and he sucked on my tongue until we were both moaning, while he slipped the hand that had been on my hip around to grab my arse. My hips snapped forwards and I shuddered when my crotch met his, both of us hard—Luke just as desperate as I, if his grunt was anything to go by.

"How long do we have?" he asked, raggedly.

I tilted my head to the side when he began to lick at the skin of my throat. "Oh, God, not nearly enough."

A low growling sound rolled up from his chest. "Then we'd better stop now. Unless you think we might have time for me to suck you off?" He swept his hand over the front of my trousers, and his smile was decidedly wicked.

"Such a *fucking* tease," I breathed, moaning in frustration when I tried to circle my hips against his hand, only to have him remove it.

"Rest assured, I will make good on every promise, spoken and unspoken, the minute I have you alone. But I'm afraid we're going to have to behave ourselves a little longer." He dropped a kiss on my neck and added, "They're coming back."

We'd barely re-taken our seats when the door opened and Trask reappeared, followed by Fisher and the other two officers, who were introduced as Detective Sergeants Matt Bennett and Andy Webster.

"Dinner will be here shortly," Trask said, resuming his own seat and glancing at Luke. "Bloody, wasn't it?"

Luke laughed sheepishly. "*Touché*, Chief Inspector."

The food arrived surprisingly quickly. Luke got his bloody steak, but had to put up with the accompanying salad. The rest of us ate Indian food—chicken tikka masala with all the sides, and drank beer from the six pack included in the delivery.

"There's something I don't understand, Chief Inspector—" I started.

"Ken, please."

I nodded. "Well, Ken, what I don't understand is, Luke and I were alone at his house all last night. Wouldn't that have been a better time for someone to come after him? I mean, they must have known where he lived — they had all his belongings, after all."

"Ah, yes, but a house like that could reasonably be expected to have a decent security system. They would have wanted to give Luke as little warning as possible. Werewolves have been known to be rather fierce when defending their territory." Trask — *Ken* — tore off a piece of naan bread and dipped it in his sauce.

"Okay, that makes sense," I replied, meal forgotten now. "But how did they know we were at the garage? I'm certain I would have noticed that tank they were driving if it had been following us."

"I can answer that," Andy Webster chipped in. He was probably the youngest of the four, with red hair and an easy smile. "When I checked our friends' mobile phones, I discovered that they'd received calls from the garage phone today, at around the time you collected your car, and last Wednesday, just after you booked it in. Someone in that garage must either be working with or being paid by the men we arrested. Matt and I are working on that."

"We're also checking out the GPS from the *tank* to find out where they've been for the last few days," Matt added, around a mouthful of food. I suppressed a shudder of distaste. Matt Bennett wasn't quite as sharply dressed or groomed as the others — his dark hair was dishevelled, his shirt rumpled and he'd spilled some sauce on his tie.

Ken laughed softly. "My wife thinks police are inquisitive, she ought to think herself lucky she didn't marry a journalist."

I felt my cheeks heat at his words, but there was playful amusement in his eyes.

"While I consider myself to be extremely lucky," Luke said, laying a hand on my arm that I could only describe as possessive. I should've felt irked. I didn't.

"Of course you do." Ken smiled, then lifted his beer in a silent toast. "As you should."

The rest of the meal was eaten while we chatted about things of little consequence. I was pleased to find that the other detectives had also read my book and weren't of a mind to have me hanged, drawn and quartered. In other circumstances I might have described it as a pleasant evening.

One of the windows had been opened a crack to help dissipate the smell of the food. It had the effect of making the traffic sounds louder. It wasn't exactly obtrusive, except for the motorbike that zoomed by. I winced at the noise, but beside me Luke stiffened and his fork fell from his fingers.

"Luke? Are you okay?" I turned in my chair to find him frowning at the window.

"I *saw* a bee."

The others followed the direction of his gaze, and Georgie got up and went to the window. She looked around and shook her head. "There's nothing there."

"I saw it," Luke insisted. "It had a broken wing." I recognised that expression—he was looking at the window, but he was seeing something else.

My own mind was whirling. There was something there, something just out of my reach. Then it hit me— Luke saw a bee, *singular*, but what he heard sounded like a *swarm*. A swarm, buzzing loudly, frighteningly loud to a man in hiding, his reality altered by drugs.

"When I was driving home that day, before I met Luke, I passed a group of motor cyclists. The noise...it sounded like a really loud *hum*. Isn't it possible that Luke heard those same bikes and mistook them for bees, bearing in mind that he was still under the influence of the drugs at the time?" Excitement made my skin prickle.

Ken seemed to consider it, and started nodding slowly. "It's possible. We'd have to establish the route they took, of course."

"They were wearing hi-vis vests with flowers on the front," I added. "There can't be many biker groups with a logo like that."

Andy wiped his mouth on a paper napkin as he was getting to his feet. "I'm on it." He left, closely followed by Matt, who grabbed a handful of onion bhajis on his way.

"But I saw, damn it, I *saw*," Luke insisted, voice rising until he was almost shouting.

I took his hands in mine. "Luke, you saw a bee, *one* bee. Don't you think you might have seen that, and heard the bikes, and maybe got the two confused in your mind?"

He frowned and shook his head, looking lost for a moment. "I don't know, maybe. It makes more sense than a swarm of bees in *November*, I suppose."

"The broken wing part is very specific, though," Georgie said, frowning. "It must mean something."

Andy strode back in then, carrying another tablet. "The bikers weren't part of a group as such, they were just friends riding together for charity. Halcyon House children's hospice in Southampton. The hospice's logo is a flower." He flipped the tablet around to show me the picture.

"A daisy, yes, that's the logo I saw."

"Okay, here's the route they took, it passes right by where you and Luke met." He showed me the screen again and I confirmed the location. There was a thrum of anticipation in the air.

"Our hoodlum friends have been quite busy in the last week," Matt said when he came back, taking the tablet Andy held out for him and tapping the screen several times. "In and out of London at least a dozen times, to Kent, Oxford and Bedford, but mostly Surrey, in particular, a place called Humblebee Farm. The place has been empty and on the market for nearly two years now, since the last owner died, and is about two miles from where Luke and Hal met. The estate agent handling the sale has this on its website." He held out the tablet for us to see. On the screen was a picture of a rundown farm, and on the sign at the gate there was a stylised honey bee, the paint fading and chipped, one wing almost completely worn away.

Luke grabbed the tablet from Matt's hands. "This is it. This is it. Hal, this is where I was held." His reaction went from elated to subdued between one breath and the next.

"They're going to be caught, Luke," I said, rubbing his back lightly. There wasn't a doubt in my mind, even if I had to do it myself, I would make sure these bastards paid for what they'd done to Luke.

He nodded and smiled, small but genuine, and the trust I saw in his eyes when he looked at me sparked something like joy in my heart.

"Okay, this is good, this is very good," Ken said, turning to Andy. "Make sure Jason hasn't left, and if he has, get him back, *now*—I want aerials of that place. They're probably long gone by now, but I want to make sure. Matt, contact Surrey police and have them keep a discreet eye on the place. No one goes in until I give the go ahead."

I had to wonder about this 'specialised unit' again. What kind of clout did they have that they could issue orders to other police services?

"Luke," Ken continued. "I'm going to arrange some police protection for you, purely as a precautionary measure and, if you're agreeable, once we're sure the farm is secured, I'd like to take you back, see if you remember anything more?"

I opened my mouth to object, but Luke settled his hand at the base of my spine. "Of course, if you think it will help," he said. I couldn't stop him from going, and I probably wouldn't even if I could, but there was no way he was going without me.

* * * *

We decided to stay in London that night, knowing that we would probably be back at the station the next day. I was a bit anxious as the car delivering us to my house in Fulham pulled into my street, but the absence of any paps or reporters outside my home settled my unease. I guessed they must have got tired of waiting around. I might have been a little miffed that my moment of fame seemed to be passing, if I wasn't so glad that there was no one to question my arrival with three uniformed police men, and an Adonis who kept looking at me like I was gourmet chocolate. I wasn't all that surprised to see my car and Luke's Land Cruiser parked outside my house— Trask's whole outfit fairly screamed efficient.

"Gents, if you would just stay down here for a moment while we check the house over." Two of them disappeared upstairs while the third, standing at parade rest and staring straight ahead, waited with Luke and me. None of them had been particularly chatty during the drive. I got the feeling they weren't very happy to be the designated babysitters.

"Will you be staying here all night?" Luke asked, his tone making it very clear that he didn't want any such thing.

The PC flicked a glance between Luke and me, and I was positive I saw colour touch his cheeks. "Our orders are to be as unobtrusive as possible, so, once we've made sure the house is secure, we'll be parked outside in the car."

I felt a bit sorry for them, then. It was hardly a dream assignment. "Are you going to be out there all night?"

"We'll be relieved by the next shift in four hours," he replied, and his cheeks turned a darker shade of pink. "But they won't disturb you."

So, he apparently thought we were going to spend the night rocking the house. I glanced at Luke, and the heat in his eyes had me wondering if perhaps we might. My gut contracted at the thought.

The heavy thump of booted feet on the stairs announced the return of our protectors. They spent a couple of minutes checking the downstairs rooms before meeting us once more in the hall.

"Everything appears to be fine. Do you have a security system, Mr Paxton?"

I nodded and indicated the white box by the door. "All in working order."

"Very good. You shouldn't have any problems, but we'll be right outside, just in case." And didn't they all look thrilled about it.

When the door closed behind them, I punched the code into the alarm box, then turned to find Luke standing so close that I actually bumped into him. The intent in his smile would have been obvious, even if he hadn't already removed his jacket and made a start on his shirt buttons.

"I believe we have unfinished business." The shirt landed on the floor beside his jacket, and in one fluid movement he swept his T-shirt over his head.

Heat flooded me, and when I spoke my tongue felt like it was too big for my mouth. "You want to do this here?" Not that I was against the idea, mind you. If we were going to rock the house, might as well start at the front door.

"Unless you want to step outside and put on a show for our police friends?" He reached for my jacket then, and shoved it down my arms. When it too was decorating the black and white tiled floor, he pushed me back against the wall and went to work on the fastenings of my trousers. "It would certainly make their job less boring."

"I'd much rather you concentrate on entertaining me." My breath was already coming in shallow pants, and the blood was rushing to my cock so fast that my vision had started to blur.

Luke dropped to his knees in front of me, grinned up the length of my body, and dragged my trousers and shorts down my legs. "I believe there was mention of me sucking you off. Would that be entertaining enough?" He wrapped one hand around my cock and swept his thumb over the tip.

"Oh, holy crap." My fingers scrabbled for purchase against the wall. "That-that would be a good place to begin."

He leaned in, swirled his tongue around the head of my dick. "Mmm, you taste good." He slid his hand down and back to cup my balls.

Managing to lock my knees so that I didn't crumple to the floor, I tilted my pelvis forwards. "It's a free bar, fill your boots."

Luke snorted, and the feel of it made me buck. He took my hips in his hands to hold me steady, then opened his mouth wider and swallowed me deep. The sensation of being surrounded by his wet warmth was almost overwhelming. My fingers curled, nails digging into the wallpaper, and a low moan fell from my lips. I was having trouble keeping my eyes open, but I desperately wanted to watch the bob of his head, the hollowing of his cheeks. His tongue was never still. It stroked along the underside of my cock, dipped into my slit when he pulled back, and teased the ridge around the head until I was practically sobbing with how fucking incredible it felt.

"Luke, *Luke*, I'm com... Oh, holy *fuck*." I tried to push at his head, but he was the original immovable object.

He continued to suck, massaging my balls, dragging his finger over the sensitive skin of my perineum, until I was shaking and begging incoherently, fingers tangled in his hair. I came with a shout that was part triumph and part shock at the intensity of the pleasure tearing through me.

While I was trying to coax my lungs to start working again, Luke quickly removed my shoes, trousers and shorts, and got up. His body pressed against mine all the way up. It made me whimper when he touched my over-sensitised dick, but it stopped me from sliding down the wall when my muscles would have given out on me.

"Entertained?" he asked, licking a stripe from my jaw to my ear.

"I-I can't feel my legs," I replied, letting my head fall back against the wall.

He laughed softly, and my skin tingled where his warm breath ghosted over it. "Then, let me feel them for you." It was such a lame joke that I had to groan.

* * * *

Morning sex was, in my humble opinion, just about the greatest invention of all time. On my hands and knees in the middle of my bed, with Luke's marvellously hard body draped over my back, his cock pounding me so hard that the headboard bounced off the wall, I was as close to Heaven as I'd ever expected to be.

Somewhere in the distance, I heard a bell ringing, but I ignored it in favour of clutching at the duvet and moaning like a whore.

"I will spend the rest of my life doing this," Luke declared, biting lightly at my shoulders, grunting with every forceful thrust. He sounded awed by the prospect.

"As long as it's with me, you'll get no argument here," I replied, voice breathy and strained. Some part of my brain was aware that I'd just made a kind of commitment, but I was prepared to offer him anything if he'd just keep hitting my sweet spot like that.

"No one else," Luke growled, biting down a little harder. "Only *you*."

Those words, the emotion behind them, and the way he wrapped his arms around my torso, one arm around my chest, the other low on my stomach, so that he wasn't putting any pressure on the bruise blooming over my ribs, was enough to tip me over the edge. Luke gave three more hard thrusts, then stilled as he poured himself into me.

We collapsed together, so tangled up that it was difficult to tell which limb belonged to which body.

And still the ringing, growing more persistent by the second. I frowned and, with no little effort, lifted my head off the pillow. "What the hell *is* that?"

Luke chuckled against my neck. "I believe that would be the doorbell, and if we don't answer it soon, I've a feeling we'll be invaded by marauding police officers."

The idea of being found like that, used and spent, should have bothered me. But what *actually* bothered me was the thought of someone else seeing Luke's naked body — that honour was now mine alone.

Chapter Ten

I pulled my scarf closer around my neck, flipped up the collar of my jacket and blew on my hands. Even gloved as they were, there was still an unpleasant tingle in my fingers, thanks to the sub-zero temperature. The grass under my feet was so brittle from the frost that it seemed to snap when I stepped on it, and an icy fog hung over the landscape, giving the bare trees and dilapidated farm house the appearance of desolation.

"Okay?" I asked Luke. His gaze was fixed on the crooked sign hanging over the gate to Humblebee Farm, his expression unreadable.

"Hmm? Oh, yes." He smiled and took my hand. "Just testing my brain to see if being here again stirs up any more memories."

"Any luck?" When he shook his head in reply I tried not to show my disappointment. I knew that he'd been pushing himself to remember everything that had happened to him during his abduction in an attempt to regain some of the control that had been stolen from him. So far all he'd remembered, besides his ultimate escape, was the pain inflicted and the fact that he'd been unable to find the crying boy—that seemed to weigh particularly heavily on him.

I squeezed his hand. "You've done so well, love, better than anyone expected." The endearment slipped out so naturally that I didn't even notice it until Luke's eyes widened, not in shock, but in undisguised pleasure.

"Thank you." What exactly he was thanking me for I didn't know, and I had no opportunity to find out when Ken and his team came to stand with us.

"Right then," Ken started, rubbing his hands together. "Jason, our resident tech genius, got us some great satellite shots of this place, including infra-red, and there are no signs of any activity, but we've brought along some backup, just in case." He indicated the two vans and the ambulance parked in the lane.

"That's a lot of backup," I said, wondering if he was expecting trouble, but not letting on. The thought disturbed me—I didn't want Luke walking into a potentially dangerous situation without warning. I decided not to ask about the ambulance.

"Only one van for backup, the other is the Scene of Crime team, they're going to comb the place for forensic evidence. Shall we?" He indicated the gate, then held a radio to his mouth. "Okay, people, I know it's a little chilly today, but you can't hide in the vans forever. Let's get a move on."

The doors to the two vans opened and at least ten people got out of each—some in police uniforms, others in the blue paper overalls of forensic scientists. *Safety in numbers*. The phrase had never seemed more appropriate. Still, I kept my hand in Luke's when he showed no signs of wanting to break the contact, and ignored the occasional *look* we got.

Luke took the lead, striding forwards with purpose and determination. With no real choice, since his grip on my hand had tightened, I fell into step beside him, lengthening my stride to keep up. The old, four-bar gate creaked and listed to the side when it was opened, swinging back to crash against the dry stone wall.

The path to the front door of the farm house was overgrown and uneven, and the door itself lay open, the locks having been forced at some point. The house smelt dank and stale, with very little light managing to get through the filthy windows. I was surprised to find most of the glass in the frames was actually intact. I felt colder inside the building than out, and wondered if it was my imagination, because I knew something of what had gone on in the place.

Luke took a deep breath, eyes closed, and his mouth turned down at the corners. The laugh lines at the edges of his eyes had been replaced with grooves, white with tension.

"This really is the place, isn't it?" I asked.

He nodded, and pointed to a door under the stairs. "You don't have—"

"I'm coming with you," I interrupted, wrapping my free hand around his arm. "You're not doing this alone, okay?"

A flash of amusement momentarily lit his eyes. "Okay. Bossy."

I smiled and turned back towards the door. "Get used to it. Now, shall we?"

Even though I could hear Ken and his team behind us, I still felt nervous about walking through that door. The stairs were narrow, so we had to finally let go of each other's hands and walk in single file. The wooden stairs had rotted in places, and groaned ominously under our weight, and the walls were damp, with mould growing in the cracks.

"Luke, it would be best if you didn't actually go into any of the rooms before forensics have had a chance to go over the place," Ken said behind us. "We need to make sure the scene isn't compromised."

Luke nodded, but said nothing. His attention was focused on an open door at the end of a narrow, low-ceilinged passageway. There was virtually no light down there, so I turned back to Ken. "Do you have a torch?" When he handed one down to me I fiddled with the switch, then squinted when the area was flooded with light. The stone floor was littered with decaying rubbish and animal faeces. Dear God, I *hoped* it was animal faeces. I had to swallow a gag of disgust.

"This is the room where I...woke up," Luke said. His tone was bland, but, with my hand resting on his back, I felt more than heard the quiver of suppressed emotion.

The room was no more awful than the rest of the house, but knowing how Luke had suffered there filled the shadowed corners with all kinds of demons. He stared for a long moment, and shook his head with a murmur of frustration—no new memories, I guessed—then turned away and moved to another door. This was the only room that had any light in it.

"Where you escaped from." It was not a question, but Luke nodded in the affirmative anyway.

"Do you recall where the boy was held, Luke?" Georgie asked, moving into the circle of torch light.

"In there, I think." Luke pointed to the third of the basement's four rooms. He moved closer and pushed the door fully open, then shut his eyes again and took a deep breath. His brow furrowed deeply and his fingers curled around the door frame.

"What is it, Luke?" I asked, moving to stand beside him.

"There's so much fear in this room. Even now, the air is thick with it." He took another breath and his voice cracked. "I-I should never have left without him. I should have *found* him."

My chest ached at the self-directed anger in his voice. "God, Luke, you were hurt and drugged, there was nothing more you could possibly have done."

"Nothing *more*? I didn't do *anything*." He spun round to face me, but the fury in his eyes faded fast and he sighed. "I'm sorry, I just…"

I lifted my hand to the cool skin of his cheek. "I know."

"This last room is empty, too," Matt said, and he sounded disappointed. Perhaps he'd been expecting the gang to be hiding out there.

"Come on, let's get some fresh air while the forensic people do their job." I nudged Luke gently towards the stairs, receiving a nod of approval from Georgie. We climbed the stairs again, and squeezed past the Scene of Crime officers bringing in their equipment. I handed the torch to one of them and followed Luke out into the weak sunlight.

"Let's take a walk, shall we?" Ken asked, as if he were suggesting a Sunday afternoon stroll in the park.

We rounded the side of the old house to an equally overgrown back garden, and woodland beyond. In a small field to the right of the house a few dozen beehives sat, broken down by disuse and the elements. We skirted the edge of the woodland until we reached a crumbling stable block, most of the roof and doors missing. In the middle of the yard was a fenced off area that I assumed had been some kind of exercise area for horses, though it looked rather small for the purpose. We moved closer to it and I noticed some dark patches staining the ground.

"What is that?" I asked. I knew nothing of horses, and hoped the answer wasn't too earthy.

Luke emitted a snarl. "It's blood. *Wolf* blood."

"Are you certain?" Ken asked, voice urgent, though it seemed like a rhetorical question, since he was already reaching for the radio in his pocket.

"Wolf blood!" Luke repeated, outrage rolling off him. He turned and stalked away, as if he couldn't bear to look anymore.

Horror dawned on me as I looked from him to the... Jesus *Christ*, was it some kind of animal pen? What the hell kind of atrocities had taken place here? I hurried after Luke while Ken barked orders into his radio.

He'd come to the edge of the woodland again by the time I'd reached him, and looked pale with rage, clenching and unclenching his hands at his sides.

"Luke, wait." His stride was long and I struggled to keep up, but I put on a burst of speed and managed to get in front of him. "Luke, please, stop."

Since his only other option was to knock me down and carry on, I was glad when he halted his progress. His expression was agonised. I felt utterly useless. "God, Luke, I-I'm sorry. It's so awful."

Without warning he pulled me into a hug so tight that I could barely breathe. My tender ribs protested the embrace, but I steadfastly ignored the pain and wrapped my arms around him. My eyes stung with unshed tears. So damn *useless*.

"You give me strength, Hal," he said, voice ragged with feeling.

I clutched at the material of his coat and struggled to get my own emotions under control. If all I could do for him was to offer him strength enough to get through this, then damn it, I would. This was no time for tears, at least, not mine.

"Whatever happened in this terrible place," I said, pulling back so that I could see his face. "It stopped because of you. The people responsible will be caught and punished because of *you*."

He sighed and laid his forehead against mine. "My Hal."

"Yes, I am." It was a simple statement. Just three words, but the most important three words I'd ever uttered, spoken with absolute clarity, free from the need to comfort, and the haze of sexual desire, from the heart rather than the groin.

Lifting his head, Luke gave me a smile that was almost beatific. But before I could do more than note the hitch in my pulse, the smile faded and his head snapped to the side. He stepped out of my arms and peered into the woodland, breathing deeply. I could practically feel the energy thrumming through him then, suddenly, he was running, vanishing into the old woods.

"What...? Luke, *wait*." For a minute I stood at the tree line, unsure of what to do. I glanced in the direction of Ken and the team, then back to where I'd last seen Luke, surprise holding me to the spot. Then I caught a glimpse of Luke, throwing his jacket aside, and without further thought I was moving, taking off after him.

There was no way I could possibly keep up with him, of course, but I pushed on, dodging low-hanging tree branches, fallen leaves crunching under my feet. I snatched up Luke's jacket when I came to it, and, a little farther on, the thick wool jumper he'd been wearing. My breathing grew laboured, and my confusion grew with every piece of clothing I retrieved—a T-shirt here, a boot there, like some odd kind of trail of breadcrumbs.

I began to slow down after a while, impeded by the bundle of clothing and the burn of freezing air in my lungs. When I finally stopped I was gasping and quite lost. I was now holding everything that Luke had been wearing, including his underwear, and had no clue as to which way to go. An icy breeze cooled the sweat that had broken out on my skin, and I shivered. What the hell was I supposed to do now? I turned round in a slow circle. Should I go back the way I'd come? Would I even be able to find my way unaided?

What about Luke—why had he taken off so abruptly? Had it been a sudden call of the wild that had pulled at him? I shook my head. No, there had been urgency in his expression, and the way he'd closed his eyes and breathed in, like he'd scented something on the air.

Anxiety twisted in my gut. I couldn't just stand there, damn it.

"*Luke*," I called at the top of my voice, and waited, straining my hearing for some kind of reply. When none was received, I tried again, then once more. But still nothing. I sighed my frustration and let my head fall back so that I was looking at the cloudless grey sky. "A little help?"

I was only a bit disappointed when there was no immediate crack of lightning to point me in the right direction, and decided that the best thing to do, to avoid becoming hopelessly lost, was to stay where I was and hope that Luke would soon return my way.

There was a fallen tree just a few feet away, so I planted myself there and settled in to wait.

Good sense lasted all of five minutes before my knee started jiggling impatiently and I had to force myself to sit still. I passed another couple of minutes by neatly folding Luke's clothes and setting them down on the tree trunk. However, when that was done, and I had nothing to occupy me but looking around and waiting for a sight or sound that seemed never to come, the disquiet grew, filling me and pushing out, like a living thing trying to break free.

I sprang to my feet and looked around me again. There was nothing in particular to guide me in one direction or another, but my gaze kept drifting to the left, so I shrugged and headed that way. Not running this time, but walking as hurriedly as I could, I took as much notice of my surroundings as possible, so that I might be able to find my way back if I had to. I quickly realised that I may as well have been walking round in circles, because, as a city boy to the bone, I couldn't tell one tree from another. But I was so anxious for a hint of Luke's presence that I kept going, tripping over roots hidden under piles of leaves, occasionally startled by the sounds of wildlife around me.

There was an ache building in my bruised ribs from all the activity, so I stopped for a minute, leant back against a tree and took several slow, measured breaths, arm held close to my side to provide some support for my ribs.

Apart from the odd scurry in the undergrowth, it was eerily quiet—the kind of quiet that was never found in the city. For a moment I longed for the roar of traffic, the screech of sirens, anything that would make me feel a little less out of my element. Then... I straightened away from the tree, suddenly alert, certain I'd heard something. For several long beats I focused entirely on listening, hoping, until...*yes*. I heard it again, a distant cry. "*Hal*" carried to me on the cold air.

Luke.

Once more, I silently pleaded, *guide me in*. A smile lifted my lips when it came, anxiety replaced by excitement. The throb in my ribs now forgotten, I took off again, tearing through the woods in his direction, heedless of the stray branches that whipped at me, catching on my clothes and stinging my cheeks. I'd no idea how far I ran or for how long, but with every step I took I could feel myself drawing closer to Luke.

When I finally saw him I stumbled to a halt, breathless and overheated. I couldn't keep the grin from my lips at the first sight of him, but it faded quickly when I saw that he was carrying something. No, some*one*. I rushed forwards again, and gasped. "The boy from the farm house?" I asked, though I already knew the answer.

Luke nodded. "I caught a hint of his scent. He was half buried under a boulder—I think he dug his way in to try and hide. Why didn't he just shift, he could have kept himself warmer?" There was no mistaking the anger mixed with concern in his tone.

"Jesus, he's freezing." I pulled off my jacket and wrapped it around the boy, who was wearing only a thin T-shirt and shorts. He was unconscious and limp in Luke's arms, his skin tinged an unhealthy shade of grey. I removed my scarf and wound it around his bare legs as best I could.

"He's hypothermic, I think," Luke said. "He has a pulse, but it's very weak. We need to get him help soon."

I nodded and we hurried back the way I'd come. "I gathered up your clothes, but I'm not sure I can find them again. Why are you naked, anyway? Wasn't one trip to the hospital this week enough for you?" I may have sounded a little more strident than I intended.

"I can shift with my clothes on, but it's murder on my wardrobe, and my senses are keener when I'm in wolf form. I had to find him. His heartbeat, it was so weak." His mouth pulled down at the corners and worry furrowed his forehead.

"Of course you had to find him." I laid a hand of apology on his arm. His skin was warmer than I'd expected, but that wouldn't last long now that he was back in his human body, I was sure. "Can you do the…scenting thing, and find your clothes? Because, I have to confess, I have absolutely no fucking idea where we are. My sense of direction relies on things like street signs and Sat Navs. If you hadn't called my name I'd never have found you."

Luke's smile was odd, deep-seated. "I didn't call your name, Hal. I did, however, *think* it."

I gasped. "Are you telling me…we can communicate, telepathically?"

"When I want you to, you will be able to hear me in your head, and I can intuit your emotions — it's a true mate thing."

True mate. The concept still felt heavy, but I noted that it was getting lighter.

"And you clearly have an exhibitionist thing." I slapped him lightly on the arse. "We're going to have to talk about that. I find I'm becoming quite possessive, and I'm not too keen on others seeing what's mine." The words were spoken in jest, an attempt to take Luke's mind off his worry for the boy.

But, I was willing to admit the truth in them, if only to myself.

Chapter Eleven

Luke watched the ambulance carrying the boy and Georgie disappear down the lane, and kept watching until the wail of the sirens faded in the distance.

"We'll go to the hospital later, Georgie promised to keep us updated." I nudged his arm to get his attention, and held up his jumper and jacket, which we'd added to the layers bundled around the boy. Luke was wearing only jeans and a T-shirt, and I could see goose bumps on the flesh of his arms. I knew he wasn't even wearing any socks under his boots, because the kid had still been wearing them when the paramedics wrapped him in one of those silver thermal blankets. "Come on, put these on before we need to call another ambulance for you."

"His heartbeat felt a little stronger there, don't you think?" he asked, pulling the thick, cable knit jumper over his head and reaching for his jacket. "I think I saw his eyelids flutter, did you see that?"

I didn't, but I nodded as I reached up to smooth down his ruffled hair. "You probably saved his life, love."

The lines in his forehead deepened. "I should never have left him here when I got out. I should have tried to find him."

"Hey, no." I grabbed the front of his jacket. "Don't do that, *please*. If you'd stayed to try to find him you might not be here now, and I-I can't tell you how much I don't like that idea. The boy is safe now. He's going to be all right, and that's because of you." *Please, God, let him be all right.*

Luke's eyes closed and he tipped his head forwards to touch our foreheads together. "We'll go and see him later," he said, and I couldn't tell if it was a question or a statement, so I just nodded.

"Everything okay, guys?" Ken asked softly.

"Yeah, we're good, right, Luke?" I leant back and fastened the buttons down the front of his wool jacket.

He glanced in the direction of the lane again, then smiled, a touch strained. "Right. What do you need me to do, Ken?"

We spent the next four hours following Ken and his team around the property, shadowed by masked forensics officers who scowled when it looked like we might touch something before them. It felt like we turned over every rock and leaf, poked around every centimetre of the crumbling out buildings, even the old chimneys and toilets were thoroughly checked out. That was one job I was thrilled not to have to perform.

As the tagged evidence bags mounted up, I could feel Luke's frustration levels rising. He had no memory of anything but the room in which he'd been held, and the fading bumblebee sign. There were indications that others had been held in the old stable block. Pieces of clothing, more blood stains, the stench of human waste and, most horrifying, chains and manacles bolted to the walls. If Luke had ever been in that place, then I would be eternally grateful to any deity listening if he never remembered.

It didn't help that there had been no news from the hospital about the boy. I tried to tell Luke that this was a good thing—no news was good news, right? He didn't seem convinced.

That, at least, was remedied when Ken received a call from Georgie at just after two in the afternoon.

"The boy's going to be okay—his name's Milo, by the way." Relief was evident in Ken's voice and the slight lessening of the white lines that had been bracketing his mouth. "Georgie said the doctor wants to keep him there for a couple of days, just to be on the safe side, but he's awake and talking, so things are looking good."

I sent up a silent prayer of thanks, and turned towards Luke in time to see his shoulders, which had been gradually creeping up to his ears, relax as some of the tension left his body. He looked at me, and gave me one of those smiles that felt intensely private and made my stomach do a little flip.

"Has he told Georgie what happened to him?" I asked.

Ken's smile faltered. "Ah, no, when I say he's talking, I mean he's answering the standard questions, you know, what's the date, the Prime Minister, and such. Georgie said he clammed up pretty quickly when she tried to ask him about this place."

"Perhaps if Luke talked to him?" I suggested, and, wincing at my presumption, turned an apologetic look on him. "I mean, if you want to?"

His smile turned reassuring, and he brushed his fingers lightly against mine. "Yes, I want to."

"It certainly might help the boy — *Milo* — to speak to someone who's been through the same trauma as him. Perhaps tomorrow, when he's a bit more rested?" Ken asked, then, without waiting for a reply, he looked at his watch. "Okay, gents, I think we've taken up enough of your time for one day. I'll get one of the lads to drive you back to the city. No doubt I'll be in touch again soon, but Luke, your help has been invaluable today."

"I wish..." Luke started, but trailed off, shaking his head. "Thank you."

Ken nodded and called Matt over. "My wife and sons are quite keen to meet you, perhaps you could come to dinner some evening — and, of course, you too, Hal?"

"Oh, uh, I'd like that," Luke said, clearly surprised. "It's a long time since I've been around other shifters. Hal?"

"Sounds good to me, you know us journos, we'll go anywhere for free food." I was already feeling lighter in spirit at the prospect of getting away from that place.

Ken laughed. "Excellent. I'll call you to set something up. Though I should warn you up front that my lovely wife firmly believes that all wolves should have a pack, or at the very least, allies. Be prepared for the recruitment speech. Matt, take Luke and Hal home, will you? And put out that cigarette, damn it. How many times have I told you that I will transfer your arse back into uniform if you don't stop that filthy habit?"

"Sorry, boss." Matt took one last, long drag from the cigarette before crushing it underfoot. "I *have* tried, but nothing seems to work for very long."

"Try again," was Ken's terse reply.

Biting back a smile, I glanced up at Luke. My amusement faded fast when I saw the expression on his face. He was suddenly deathly pale, his eyes wide, and he didn't appear to be breathing at all. Alarm bells immediately sounded in my head, and a cold fist of apprehension gripped me.

"Luke, what is it? What's wrong?" I moved to stand in front of him and lifted my hands to his face, but didn't touch him, afraid of startling him.

"He-he was trying to quit," Luke said quietly, almost to himself.

I cast a quick glance at Ken and frowned. He shrugged. "Matt's trying to stop smoking, yes, why is that so important?" I asked. I laid a hand on his chest. He seemed so far away at that moment that I felt the need to reassure myself of his physical presence.

Blinking, he shook his head. "No, not Matt...not Matt." He looked in the direction of the animal pen, sucked in a sharp breath and staggered backwards. "Oh, my God."

I grabbed hold of the front of his jacket to steady him, but my own insides were churning with an awful feeling of foreboding. Luke's face was bloodless, and the desolation in his voice made me colder than the November wind. "Luke..." Before I could say another word, he shook off my hands and headed for the pen on legs that looked a little unsteady.

From behind him, I could see the deep movement of his shoulders as he breathed heavily. He slumped forward and rested his hands on his thighs, and I rushed towards him, afraid that he was about to pass out. He dropped to his knees just as I reached him, and when I crouched before him and took his hand, my heart beating out a fierce tattoo in my chest, he grabbed hold and clutched so hard that it verged on painful. Ken and Matt moved to stand quietly behind Luke.

"This place" — Luke gestured to the pen — "it's not, it *wasn't* a holding pen, it was a ring, for fighting."

"Fighting? You mean, like some kind of sport?" I asked, frowning.

He shook his head vigorously and surged to his feet, taking me with him courtesy of the grip he still had on my hand. "No, this was no sport. The wolves…they were forced to shift, forced to fight. To the death."

"Dear God, that's…" *Sickening, unbelievable, horrifying* — there were no words to adequately convey the disgust I felt. "But how do you know this?"

"Because I remember," Luke replied, his tone equal measures of relief and dismay. "I remember everything. Paper. I need paper, and something to draw with."

Ken quickly fished a notebook from the inside pocket of his coat, and handed it over with a silver pen. Luke let go of my hand, flipped open the notebook and began to sketch something with rapid sweeps of his hand.

"There was a man," he said, as he continued to draw. "He would come into the room where it was being held, usually accompanied by a couple of thugs. He told me that it was only a matter of time before they broke me — like they'd broken the others — I could resist all I wanted, but sooner or later I would be in the ring fighting for my life. He was trying to stop smoking, kept popping that nicotine gum."

It was amazing, really, that something so small should be the key to unlocking Luke's memories. My amazement was, however, fleeting, quickly replaced by a wave of revulsion. "Like some twisted fight club."

Luke nodded, but kept his focus on the page in front of him. "They find wolves with no pack, nobody to miss them, then they starve, beat, drug them—anything it takes to break their spirit—and put them in the ring together to fight it out."

"So, the bodies found were the losers in these fights?" Ken asked. I couldn't tell if he was more furious or sickened.

"There will be more that haven't been discovered—they've been doing this for a long time." Luke's hand stopped moving, but he just stared at the notebook, as if trying to digest the enormity of his own words. He closed his eyes for a second, then handed the book back to Ken. "This is the man, the one who was running it all."

I looked over Ken's shoulder at the picture—an incredibly detailed drawing of a good-looking man, with wide-set eyes, a sharp jaw line and neatly trimmed goatee.

"He's probably in his thirties," Luke added, twirling the pen between his fingers now. "With dark hair and brown eyes—deep brown."

"This is fantastic," Ken said, digging his phone out of his pocket and taking a photograph of the sketch. He then hit a speed dial button and held the phone up to his ear. "Jason, I'm sending you a picture. Do your stuff and try to find out who this guy is."

"I'll be back in a minute," Matt said, and strode off towards the vans parked in the lane.

I turned to Luke while Ken finished his phone call. "Are you all right?"

"Honestly, I-I don't know," he replied, and took a step closer to me, so that our hands were brushing together again. "On the one hand, I'm glad that the fog has lifted, but on the other..."

"You're not keen on the view," I guessed, and his lips quirked in a half smile. I couldn't begin to imagine how he must have been feeling right then. For myself, I was torn between wanting to punch someone in the throat, and the need to protect this giant of a man who had already survived too much in his life. I wrapped my fingers tightly around his arm.

His eyes locked with mine, and he smiled. It was like a blast of warmth in the frigid temperature. "Although, the view right now is as close to perfection as I've ever dreamed of finding."

As inappropriate as the circumstances were, the heat of arousal settled in my gut. I would probably have flushed, at both the naked appreciation in his eyes, and my own reaction to it, but for the fact that every drop of blood in my body that wasn't actively keeping me alive, had rushed south to pool hotly between my legs. I tore my gaze from his, and stared at the dirt between my feet as I tried to get my suddenly ragged breathing under control.

"Boss." Matt returned then, carrying a clear evidence bag with a blister pack inside—the type used for medicines, or, in this case, nicotine gum. "This was found in the kitchen at the farm house—I remembered seeing one of the forensics guys bag it."

Ken grinned. "Along with a million other pieces of apparently worthless crap. Thank the Lord for nit-picking scientists." There was a gleam in his eye when he looked at us, like he was enjoying the challenge of the puzzle on some level most civilians would probably never understand. As someone who'd made a career of seeking out puzzles to solve, I understood only too well. "Okay, lads, why don't you head on home, and we'll talk tomorrow?"

"My car's just over here," Matt said, leading the way. There was a little bounce to his step that was oddly endearing, like a small boy who'd won his big brother's respect.

Luke handed the pen back to Ken, and dropped his hand to the dip at the base of my spine. Even through layers of winter clothing, I could feel the warmth of his touch and, without conscious thought, I found myself leaning into him. I still wasn't entirely convinced about this whole *bond* thing, but I couldn't deny that I seemed to be hyperaware of his presence beside me, like all my senses were heightened around him. It was more than new relationship euphoria — there was something almost visceral about my reaction to him. I'd never experienced anything like it before, and I wanted to keep it.

The journey back to my place took just over half an hour, and most of it was made in silence, except for the classic pop radio Matt had tuned in. Luke stared out of the side window for almost the entire trip, but he kept his hand wrapped around mine, occasionally brushing his thumb over my knuckles. Only the tightness at the corners of his mouth hinted at the direction of his thoughts.

"What the hell?" Matt's exclamation pulled me from my own thoughts, and I looked up to find that we'd turned into my street, and that there was a welcoming committee of photographers and reporters waiting outside my house.

Annoyance rose fast and fierce. "*Jesus Christ*. Do these people not have fucking lives of their own?"

"What is it?" Luke asked, suddenly alert. He followed my gaze to the gathering and frowned. "Why are those people outside your house, Hal?"

"Because, apparently, I am endlessly fucking fascinating," I bit out, and immediately regretted my tone when Luke flinched. "I'm sorry. It's...let's just get inside, okay?"

Still looking a touch confused, he nodded.

Matt pulled the car up outside my gate and we were instantly surrounded. "Want me to flash my ID at them and clear a path?" he asked.

"God, no, it will just give them more questions, but thanks." I turned to Luke to find he was watching the people outside the car through narrowed eyes.

"Wait here," he said, and it sounded like an order, but before I could take exception to that, he was out of the car, pushing his way through the crowd, and opening my door.

As I got out of the car he put himself between me and the reporters clamouring for sound bites, practically fucking growling when anyone got too close. I have to admit it was pretty damn funny—and way hotter than it had any right to be. With Luke as my own personal wall, I was able to get to my front door without too much hassle.

"Hal, what's your reaction to the Home Secretary announcing a public enquiry into the Met?"

"Do you think the police Commissioner should give in to pressure and resign?"

"Hal, is it true you're dating Keira Knightly?"

The voices blended together until there was just a cacophony of near incoherent noise. I fumbled with my keys to get the door open, and when a mic was suddenly thrust in my face, Luke grabbed it, shoved the owner aside and snarled, "*Back off*" before tossing the mic into the street.

"What the hell was that?" he asked the minute we were inside the house with the door firmly closed.

"*That* has been my life for longer than I care to remember, although I had thought it was starting to lose steam," I replied, striding into the living room, where I turned on the TV and clicked to the news channel to find out why this shit storm had suddenly picked up again. And there it was, *damn it*, my face on television again, being credited for that morning's announcement of a public enquiry by the Home Secretary. The police Commissioner was adamantly refusing to step down, but the news pundits were as good as taking bets on how long the man would remain at his desk. I slumped down on the sofa, shaking my head in disbelief. "I can't do this again."

The sofa dipped beside me and Luke wrapped his arm around my shoulder. "Go and pack a bag, you're coming home with me." He dropped a kiss on top of my head, then nudged me to move.

"I'm not sure I like you giving me orders," I said, even as I got to my feet.

He grinned, unrepentant. "You love it. Now, go and pack."

"Yes, sir!" I tossed off a two fingered salute and headed for the door, amusement bubbling up inside me.

"Oh, and, Hal?" I turned round to find him watching me with a cocked eyebrow and twitching lips. "Keira Knightly?"

"Fuck you," I retorted, and felt my cheeks heat.

His smile widened. "We'll see."

I walked upstairs slowly, because the erection suddenly pushing at the front of my trousers wouldn't allow for anything else.

Chapter Twelve

I'd always thought of myself as a fairly cerebral person, never one to be carried away by passion, or distracted by a pretty face—at least, not for long. So it came as something of a surprise to me—though, far from unpleasant—that just days after meeting Luke, I found myself becoming increasingly, wonderfully, addicted to all things carnal. The way Luke's big hands gripped my hips—blunt nails digging into the top of my arse while his thumbs moved in small circles in the dips of my pelvis. The raw heat in his eyes as he looked up at me from where he was lying back against the pillows, hair a spill of gold on the dark blue cotton of the pillow case. The sweep of his tongue over lips gone puffy from kissing, leaving them moist and oh so inviting. And, oh, my God, the feel of his cock buried deep inside me, thick and pulsing…it was like a fucking religious experience.

My thighs burned as I moved up and down on his shaft, toes curling and fingers pressing into the hard contours of his abs as wave after wave of pleasure washed over me.

"This…oh, fuck, this is f-fast becoming my very favourite thing to do," I gasped, and blinked a bead of sweat out of my eye when it rolled down from my forehead. "I-I've been meaning to get a new hobby."

Luke barked a laugh. "Beats the hell out of trainspotting." He rocked his hips, and unerringly nailed my prostate like it was a sport, and he was a fucking Olympic champion.

"Better exercise too." Every muscle in my body strained and quivered. A keening moan escaped me when Luke removed a hand from my hip, brought it to his mouth and licked it before wrapping it around my dick and setting up a slow, teasing motion. "Really gets the heart…pumping. Oh, holy fuck, *faster*."

"Such a dirty mouth," Luke said, lifting his other hand to run the tips of his fingers over my lips. I immediately sucked two into my mouth and laved them, as his pupils blew wide and his hips stuttered. "I fucking love that."

I picked up speed, ignoring the protests of muscle and sinew, and rode him hard and fast while his hand sent me careening over the edge. Tumbling forwards onto his chest, I was aware of the hot rush of his own release, and smiled in satisfaction when I felt the rapid, uneven beat of his heart under my cheek.

"I'm going to buy this house," Luke said, after a long time of simply stroking my back in silence.

I lifted my head, and rested my chin on my fist to look at him. "Really? What brought that on?"

Still trailing his fingers idly along my spine, he shrugged—not as nonchalantly as he'd aimed for, I guessed. "Ever since I…left home, I've been something of a nomad, never staying in any place long enough to kick the dust off my shoes. But I like it here. I think I could make my home here."

Was there added weight to his tone when he said that? Was I imagining it? Hoping, perhaps? I lifted my free hand to his cheek and rubbed my thumb over the vulnerable skin under his eye. "You should have a real home, you deserve it."

He turned his head to place a light kiss on my palm, then reached for the quilt and pulled it over us. "Sleep, it's been a long day."

That was one order that was very easy to follow. I was already pleasantly boneless, and my eyelids soon gave up any attempt at remaining open.

* * * *

"So, who's the babe?" my mum asked, when I phoned her the next morning to reassure her that I was okay, in spite of my face being plastered all over the front pages of the papers.

I didn't try to hide my amusement. "*Babe*, Mum, really?" I glanced at the newspapers spread out over the top of the kitchen island, my lover looking gorgeously ferocious in most of them.

She snorted indelicately. "Darling, I'm not blind, that man is a hunk. Now, tell me, who is he? The papers don't say."

"His name's Luke, and he's..." What exactly? My lover, yes, but I wasn't telling her *that*. My soul mate — that was still under investigation. I wandered over to the patio doors, leaned against the frame, and watched Luke, in his wolf form, prowling around the garden, all sleek elegance and restrained power. My future? Dear God, I hoped so.

"Special?" Mum asked gently, when I forgot to answer.

I smiled sheepishly, even though she couldn't see me. "Yes. It's still new, but...yes."

In the silence that followed, I could see her in my mind, standing there in our kitchen at home, hand on her heart, and a goofy smile on her face. "I'm very happy for you, love," she said it calmly, but I heard the underlying excitement in her voice.

As I watched, Luke shifted back into his human form, the transformation as fluid and beautiful as a well-choreographed dance. He saw me and headed in, gloriously naked. When he drew closer I was able to see the smile on his lips, the gleam in his eye. For me. A thrill ran through my body. "Me too, Mum, me too."

"You must bring him for Christmas—he's not a vegetarian, is he? I've only just mastered the turkey thing, I don't think I could manage nut cutlets or tofu, which, if you ask me, just looks like a lump of rubber."

I covered the mouthpiece with my hand when Luke came up the steps to the patio. "My mum—she wants you to come for Christmas dinner."

He grinned and nodded, then dropped a kiss on my forehead.

"He'd love to come, Mum, and no, he's not a vegetarian." I bit back a laugh when Luke glanced back over his shoulder and pulled a horrified face at that. "I have to go now, Mum, give my love to Dad."

"Okay, sweetheart, you take care of yourself, and your young man too."

I ended the call, put my phone down and turned to see Luke coming out of the laundry room just off the kitchen, zipping the fly on a pair of jeans and carrying a black T-shirt. "Oh, you dressed."

Snickering at my obvious unhappiness, he pulled the T-shirt over his head. The way it moulded to his perfect torso somewhat mitigated my disappointment. He crossed the kitchen, the bottoms of his jeans brushing against his bare feet—and really, when were bare feet enough to give me a hard on? It was like, in getting to know Luke, I was also learning more about myself.

"I thought you had...issues with my 'exhibitionist streak'?" He crowded me against the island, tilted his hips against mine and arched an eyebrow when he felt the hard press of my arousal.

"Only when we're not alone," I replied, and smoothed my hands up over his abs to his chest, where I pinched one nipple through the thin cotton, and smiled at the gasp it elicited. "Otherwise, please don't feel under any obligation to modesty."

His eyes shone with a mixture of amusement and desire, the latter I also felt stirring against my stomach. "How very magnanimous of you. Perhaps we should institute a house rule—leave your clothes at the door, unless we have company."

"That could get a little chilly," I said, even as heat began to seep into my body.

"Oh, I doubt that very much," he replied, and lowered his head to capture my lips in a hard, wet kiss that made me shiver with barely repressed need. When, all too soon, he lifted his head, I saw regret in his expression. "We're about to have guests."

I didn't ask how he knew that, nor did it surprise me when the intercom buzzer sounded just seconds later. "We should continue this discussion later—I may need a bit of convincing on the no clothes thing," I said.

Luke grinned as he stepped out of my arms. "I believe I can come up with an argument or two to back up my suggestion," he said, and before he turned away he dropped his hand so that his knuckles dragged over the bulge in the front of my trousers.

"You'd fucking better!"

The sound of his laughter rang in my ears, and as he went to answer the intercom, I moved to stand in front of the fridge with the door open, in an attempt to cool my ardour, muttering about blue balls and cock teases.

When Luke let them in a few minutes later, Ken and Georgie brought with them a cold blast of winter air, and matching expressions of such seriousness I felt a stab of misgiving. Luke obviously felt it too, because all trace of humour left him and he scowled.

"What's wrong?" he asked with quiet intensity. "Did something happen to the boy?"

Ken immediately held up his hands, palms out, and shook his head. "No, no, he's fine. Better than fine, actually. They've moved him out of intensive care and he's walking around. He's eager to meet you, to thank you for helping him."

A shadow of regret passed over Luke's features, but he smiled and nodded. "I'll go and see him this afternoon."

The two detectives exchanged a look I couldn't decipher, but it didn't exactly fill me with optimism.

"Why don't we sit and talk, Luke?" Ken suggested.

"Sure, we can use the living room. Why don't you and Georgie go on through, and Hal and I will bring coffee? It's the second door on the left." It may have sounded like a question, but everyone in the room knew it wasn't. After just a moment of hesitation, Ken and Georgie left the kitchen. Their footsteps echoed on the floor, then vanished onto the thick carpet of the living room.

"What's going on?" I asked Luke as he took four mugs down from the cupboard. The coffee pot was already full and hot. I took a tray from under the island and placed the sugar bowl and spoons on it.

"They're very anxious about something," Luke said, adding the mugs to the tray. "Especially Georgie – I could smell the stress pouring off her even before I opened the door."

"Well, I guess there's only one way to find out." I reached for the coffee things, but Luke stopped me, cupped my cheek with one hand and leaned in to touch his lips to mine in a kiss that was so tender and soft that I barely felt the contact. When I looked up at him he just smiled.

"After you."

Ken and Georgie were sitting on one of the forest green sofas that flanked the limestone fireplace. A low coffee table sat between the two sofas, but Ken was busily spreading photographs out on it, so Luke moved a small side table closer for me to set down the tray.

"What's this?" Luke asked, taking a seat opposite the detectives. When I would have started filling the mugs with coffee, he reached out, took my hand, and tugged gently until I was sitting beside him.

"I need you to take a look at these pictures, Luke," Ken said without preamble. I noticed then just how tired he was looking. There were dark circles under his eyes, and that little spark of humour he always seemed to carry was nowhere to be seen. "Tell me if you recognise anyone."

"Oh, mug shots?" Luke leaned closer to the table, and his head moved slowly from one side to the other as he studied the photos. After a few seconds, he stabbed one with his finger. "This one. He's the one who was running things."

I looked at it—the sketch Luke had made at the farm might have been copied from the photograph he'd just picked out, the likeness was so close.

"You're certain?" Ken asked. Was that a hint of excitement in his voice?

Luke's eyes never moved from the picture. "I saw this man perhaps five or six times, and every time, I got the crap beaten out of me by his pet thugs, stabbed with a hypodermic needle or zapped with a stun gun, usually all three. He's the one."

I blanched at the words and tightened my fingers where they rested on his thigh. Luke sat back again and wrapped his hand around mine.

"Okay," Ken said, and picked up the photo. He gave Georgie a brief nod, and she left the room, punching a number into her phone. "This is the same man Milo picked out last night."

"Who is he?" I asked, finding some comfort in the sweep of Luke's thumb over my hand. Or, maybe it was just the contact. I was quickly discovering that everything felt a little better when I was touching him.

Ken tidied away the photos. "His name is Robert Doubleday."

The name rang a bell in my head, and I frowned as I tried to remember… "Oh, my God. Doubleday—he was the founder of Prime Order."

"That was Victor Doubleday," Ken confirmed. "Robert's father. It seems that Robert holds many of the same beliefs as his father. With independent identifications from both Luke and Milo, we have enough to get a search warrant for all property owned by Robert Doubleday"—he pointed over his shoulder—"Georgie's getting the ball rolling on that now."

"Then what?" Luke asked.

Ken pursed his lips and tapped the pile of photos against his knee, before dropping them onto the table and getting to his feet. "The Home Secretary himself has taken a keen interest in this case—to the point where he wants daily progress updates," he said, moving to stand in front of the fireplace, hands in the pockets of his trousers. At first glance he looked relaxed enough, but the tense set of his shoulders told another story. "Apparently, our new Prime Minister is an advocate of shifter rights. For the last few months, since taking office, she has been quietly gathering support for her Shifter Protection Bill. She wants to make crimes against shifters a hate crime, and outlaw groups like Prime Order that actively advocate violence against werekind. She hopes to have the bill passed soon, very soon."

The misgiving I'd felt in the kitchen was twisting into a deeper sense of dread that I couldn't explain. "What does this have to do with Luke?"

"The Home Secretary's greatest fear has been that the new bill would bring about a resurgence of the...troubles we saw at the millennium," Ken explained. He'd started pacing in front of the hearth. I got the feeling that he was running on nervous energy at this point. "If we find enough evidence to link Robert Doubleday—and by extension, Prime Order— to the deaths of these young werewolves, the prosecution will be expedited in the hope of a guilty verdict around the same time as the bill coming before Parliament. The Home Secretary believes, and I must say that I tend to agree with him on this, that when details come out about what happened to Luke and

Milo, and those other young men, the true, violent, hate-filled nature of Prime Order will be revealed. People will see them for what they are, and the support that has been dwindling over the last few years will be further lost."

I'd been a journalist long enough to know when someone was avoiding answering a question. This behaviour from Ken, a man I'd very quickly come to respect for his obvious intelligence, integrity and compassion, set my nerves on edge. What was he trying *not* to tell us?

"Ken," I started, but said nothing more until he stopped moving and looked at me. "What does this actually mean for *Luke*?"

Indecision flashed across the man's face before Ken sighed and resumed his seat on the sofa, though he looked far from comfortable perched right on the edge with his elbows resting on his knees. "Am I wrong to assume that you will be prepared to stand up in court and testify against Robert Doubleday, Luke?"

"What? No, of course not," Luke replied sharply, clearly surprised that there should be any doubt.

Ken nodded. "Prime Order isn't what it once was. As I said, its membership has been falling steadily over the years, but there are still some zealots who hold fast to Victor Doubleday's convictions that the integration of werekind is opening the door to the subjugation and ultimate extinction of humanity."

"So, not insane at all," Luke said with a bark of laughter that showed just how ridiculous he thought it was.

I found it considerably less funny. I had a pretty good idea where this was going, and finally understood the distress that had been gnawing at me since Ken and Georgie's arrival.

"Insane enough that the second we arrest Robert Doubleday, you will become a target," Ken retorted. "You...and Milo."

Luke's smile died on his lips. "You can protect him though, right?"

"Of course, but to protect Milo, and safeguard the case against Doubleday, we must also protect you." Ken was back on his feet again, but this time there was a definite sense of purpose about him.

"I don't..." Luke tilted his head to the side, puzzled.

My heart sank. "He wants to put you in witness protection."

Chapter Thirteen

"Witness protection?" Luke asked. "You mean like in the movies, with a new name and a new life, all that?"

Ken shook his head, spreading his hands in a way that I guessed was meant to be conciliatory. "It wouldn't be the full supergrass experience. We'd move you and Milo to a safe house with police protection until the trial—"

"And Hal," Luke inserted, and I felt him move closer to me.

"Ah." Ken tucked his hands into his pockets and rocked on the balls of his feet. "That might be...inadvisable."

"What do you mean?" Luke asked, the timbre of his voice low, cautionary.

Ken sighed. "Hal's profile has been too high recently to allow for anonymity. If we place you together and someone recognises Hal, it could be dangerous for everyone involved."

Something squeezed my chest at Ken's words, and I found myself leaning into the warmth of Luke's body, grateful when he tightened his arm around me.

"That's not possible. I won't be separated from Hal," he declared, tone and posture screaming defiance.

"For the sake of your safety, Luke…" Ken began, but Luke shook his head sharply.

"No. I *cannot* be separated from Hal. It will…weaken me. If you don't understand that, then ask your wife to explain."

Ken opened his mouth to argue, but I held up my hand to stay his words and turned in my seat so that I could look directly at Luke. There was suddenly a lump in my throat, and when I spoke my voice sounded thin and strained.

"Luke, maybe you should listen to him. It wouldn't be for long, would it?" I asked Ken.

"Perhaps a couple of months," he replied.

My insides twisted until I felt nauseated, but I forced myself to smile at Luke. "A couple of months to ensure your safety, and Milo's, that's not so long." So why did I feel like I was being turned inside out?

But Luke shook his head again, the light of determination glinting in his eye as he turned to Ken. "And what about Hal? He saw the men at the garage, doesn't that put him at risk?"

"Low level thugs," Ken replied. "We can get them on possession of the stun gun alone, without Hal's testimony. With their records they're looking at prison time."

"Can't you make some kind of deal with them? Offer them their freedom in exchange for this Doubleday?" Luke asked. His hand on my thigh was now gripping painfully tight, but I made no attempt to dislodge it. Any connection with him at that moment seemed vital to me.

"They won't give him up—they'd rather serve time than be labelled informants. No, our best and only way to get Doubleday is if you and Milo testify."

A muted growl rumbled up from Luke's chest, and he stood. "You'll have my testimony, but on *my* terms. This house is as secure as anything you could provide. Milo and Hal will come and stay here with me. I'll protect them both."

"Wait, now," I said, moving to stand beside Luke, bristling a little at his high-handedness. "You can't make decisions like that for me. I'm a grown man and perfectly capable of taking care of myself."

Luke's expression was one of genuine surprise. "You're my mate—it's my duty and my honour to protect you. I don't mean to belittle you in any way." He looked...*hurt*, and I instantly wanted to apologise, but found myself laughing instead.

"I'm never going to be able to stay angry at you, am I?"

Luke grinned. "Oh, we'll fight, my Hal, I'll enrage you and you'll make me grovel for forgiveness, and we'll make up and it will be *glorious*."

The idea of Luke grovelling before anyone was too ridiculous for words, so I turned to Ken and shrugged. "I guess it's decided."

Ken's lips thinned with annoyance. "Milo's not your mate, he's not even part of your pack. You can't make this decision for him."

The smile slipped from Luke's lips and he nodded. "He must make his own decision, of course. We'll give him his options and let him choose."

Ken took a deep breath and closed his eyes, as if trying to keep calm, then a clearly reluctant smile tugged at one corner of his mouth. "Bloody werewolves. I suppose I can get a security detail to guard here as well as anywhere else."

"That's the spirit," Luke teased.

"Is it okay for us to go and see Milo now?" I asked.

Ken cocked an eyebrow. "Could I possibly stop you? Yes, it should be fine. We won't be raiding Doubleday's premises until dawn—assuming we can get the paperwork sorted out."

"What more do you know of him—Milo, I mean?" Luke asked, all humour faded.

"He's a poor little bugger, from what we can gather," Ken said, a sympathetic twist to his features. "Sixteen years old, he was abandoned as a baby and bounced from one foster home to another until the system cut him loose four months ago. He was staying in a bedsit and working at a supermarket until last month. His landlord thought he'd taken off and gave his room away—Georgie's going over there this afternoon to collect his things."

"So, they had him for a month," Luke rumbled, eyes narrowing.

Ken nodded. "He was malnourished, but there was no sexual abuse and no drugs in his system. If they beat him, he'd healed before you found him. He's still reluctant to talk about what happened at the farm."

"What hospital have they taken him to?" I asked, sensing that Luke was eager to get moving.

Ken took his notebook and pen from the inside pocket of his coat and scribbled something, then tore out the page and handed it to me. "The hospital and ward number. I'll have an officer accompany you, just to be on the safe side."

When he received no argument, Ken smiled and took his leave, after making us promise to wait until one of his officers came to collect us. Luke and I followed him to the door, and when the car carrying Ken and Georgie reached the front gate, Luke pressed the release button to let them out. He waited until the gate closed again before shutting the door.

"You're not angry with me, are you?" Luke asked, catching my hand and pulling me to him.

I shook my head and laid my free hand on his chest. "No, I'm not angry, I was just…taken aback, I guess. I've been making my own decisions for a long time now. I'm not sure I can hand over control like that. I'm not even sure I want to."

Luke pushed his fingers through my hair and brought his hand around to my cheek. "I'm not trying to control you, Hal, but, as a werewolf, there are certain things that are part of my genetic makeup. The most important thing to me is, and must be, the safety of my mate and my pack. I've never been in this situation before, and I just reacted without considering things first."

"I guess this is new for both of us," I said, leaning into his caress. "We can feel our way through it together."

"I like the sound of that," Luke said with a theatrical leer, and pulled me closer.

Fire bloomed fast and hot inside me. "Tell me something, are all werewolves so bloody randy?" I pressed my hips against his to remove any sting from the words.

Luke's pupils dilated and he dropped his hands to my arse, using the leverage to grind our hardening cocks together. "I'm of an earthy, instinctual race, my Hal. We have feelings and emotions and we act upon them. We're not entirely uncivilised, but we don't hide behind a manufactured veneer of propriety."

I licked suddenly dry lips and watched Luke's gaze follow the movement of my tongue. "So, basically, you see, you want..."

He slid his hand up under my shirt and I shivered, eyelids drooping.

"I *take*," he finished, and lowered his head to capture my mouth in a hot, wet and bruising kiss that made my head spin.

* * * *

Detective Andy Webster arrived to drive us to the hospital an hour later. As we were getting into the car I noticed a tell-tale bulge in the line of his jacket, and my eyes widened in surprise.

"Are you *armed*?"

Andy smiled, and shit, he looked far too young and fresh-faced to be carrying a concealed weapon.

"The boss thought it prudent."

My head buzzed. Now guns were involved, and everything felt so *real*. "And you can just do that, strap on a gun?"

The smile became a grin, and Andy winked. "We're a specialised unit."

"Yes, I heard that," I said, and got into the back of the car with Luke.

"You're upset," Luke said, turning concerned eyes on me.

My internal organs felt like they were tumbling over each other, in as much of a turmoil as my mind. "I just had a dose of reality," I said, and tried without success to laugh it off. I took Luke's hand in mine and laced our fingers together. "Someone might actually try to hurt you."

He squeezed my hand and touched his forehead to my temple. "They may try, but they won't succeed." I wished I felt half as sure as he sounded.

The rhythmic sweep of Luke's thumb across the back of my hand had a calming, almost hypnotic effect. By the time we reached the hospital half an hour later, I felt more tranquil.

Andy remained outside Milo's room with the two uniformed officers on duty.

Curled up in a chair, reading a book, Milo Brant was small for his age, with soft features that spoke of a boy on the cusp of manhood. He jumped when we opened the door to his room, and turned to us with wide, frightened eyes that seemed too big for his thin face. But the fear quickly disappeared, replaced by a shy smile.

"Luke?" he asked, closing his book and setting it down on his blanket-covered lap.

"That's me," Luke said, voice gentle. "This is Hal, my mate. How are you feeling today?"

"Okay," Milo answered, then lowered his head, smile fading. "They, uh, they say I can leave soon."

It wasn't hard to figure out what he was thinking. Small as it had been, his life had been shattered—he had no home to go to, and no job with which to support himself. My heart went out to him.

"We wanted to talk to you about that, Milo," Luke said, sitting on the side of the bed and drawing me close. "Detective Chief Inspector Trask has indicated that you want to testify against the men who did this to us?"

Milo lifted a hand to his mouth and began to chew on his thumb nail. His nod of affirmation was far from resolute.

"It looks like the trial will be expedited" — Milo frowned at that, so Luke explained — "the process will be sped up so that the trial happens quicker than usual. Now, we already know that these are bad people, so there's a...small chance that they might try to get to us so that we can't give evidence against them."

Milo's eyes went wide and he clutched his book to him like a shield. Luke leaned over and laid a hand on the boy's shoulder. "We have a couple of options open to us, Milo," Luke said. I liked the way he said *we* and *us*, so that Milo wouldn't have to feel alone in this. I had the feeling the boy had spent more than enough time isolated.

"What's that?" Milo asked quietly.

Luke withdrew his hand, but continued to lean towards Milo. "Detective Trask thinks it would be a good idea to move us to a safe house until the trial is complete. He'd give us round the clock security."

"What's the other option?"

For a few seconds, Luke said nothing. He looked at me, as if asking a question, and I nodded — yes, I agreed that we would be safe together at Luke's house. I saw gratitude in his eyes.

"I have a house, Milo, out in the country. It has a good security system, and if we all choose to stay there together, the police can offer extra protection."

"I can...I can stay with you, at your house?" The hope, the fear of hope, in Milo's voice brought a sting to the back of my eyes.

"If that's what you want," Luke said. "But you might feel better in Detective Trask's safe house."

I found myself holding my breath waiting for Milo's answer. If he chose the safe house, would Luke go with him? The thought made me ache — I'd only just found him, how could I let him go again so soon? But the alternative was Milo alone, again.

Milo shook his head and blushed. "No, I feel safe with you. You're big and strong, an Alpha," he said, as if that explained everything, and perhaps, for werekind, it did.

"Then that's what we'll do." Luke smiled reassuringly, and Milo seemed to relax. I found the next breath easier to draw.

"Thank you for finding me," Milo said. "They told me I might have frozen to death if I stayed out there much longer."

"Milo, why didn't you shift?" Luke asked, tone rich with curiosity, but no judgement. "You could have run farther, faster."

Embarrassed colour suffused Milo's face and he lowered his head again. When he spoke I had to strain my ears to hear him. "I-I was frightened, and I can't...when... I don't have a lot of control over it."

Without thinking, I moved to crouch beside him. "What happened to you was terrible, Milo, it's only natural to be afraid. But you got away, on your own."

He shook his head and his shaggy brown hair fell over his face. "They didn't hurt me the way they hurt the others. I... They made me..." He'd started to tremble, so I put my hand on his arm, sending a warning glance to Luke, should he decide to object.

The look he gave me fairly screamed *what*? I rolled my eyes and turned back to Milo.

"What did they make you do, Milo?" I coaxed.

I only realised he was crying when his shoulders started to shake. I sunk to my knees beside the chair and put my arm around him. He resisted for a moment before giving in to the need for comfort.

"I helped them," he croaked, and a tear splashed onto his forgotten book.

"Oh, God." I pulled him closer, and Luke dropped to his knees in front of him.

"But not willingly, I think," Luke said, and there was no doubt in his tone. "They made you."

Milo nodded shakily, and looked up at us from under his mess of hair. "The leader, the one they called *Guv*, he was angry when they brought me in, said I was too small—no use to man nor beast. But they found a use for me. There were three other shifters there before they brought you in, Luke. Their spirits were broken by beatings and drugs, and when they tried to put up any resistance they had that *Taser* thing used on them, over and over again. They'd been practically starved for weeks, but when they finally agreed to fight the drugs were stopped so that they were able to shift again, and they were allowed some food and water—I brought it to them. The Guv said he wouldn't let a human lower himself to serve a-a beast."

Curving his big hand around Milo's, Luke sighed and touched his forehead to the boy's. "Then the only ones you helped were the shifters, Milo, you brought them food and water they might otherwise never have had."

"It didn't do them any good, though," Milo said, bitterness lacing his tone. "They're dead now, all three of them."

Luke closed his eyes, but not before I saw a flash of anger in them. "How did they die, Milo?"

All colour left the boy's face, and he clasped his hands together in a vain attempt to hide the way they shook. "There was a fight, it was horrible. About a dozen men with lots of money making bets on which shifter would live and which would die. I was made to bring the men drinks—my ankles were in chains at those times, to make me look like a slave, I think."

The story made me feel ill, and I could see on his face the battle Luke was having to keep his rage at bay.

"By the end of the fight the shifters were shredded and bloody… So much blood." His voice was distant, and I hugged him tighter in an attempt to keep him in the present. Only one was allowed to live, but they refused to go in for the kill. The Guv took out a gun and loaded it with two silver bullets. He told them that one of them would die at the other's hands, or they would both die by his. The men…they *cheered* as one of the shifters ripped out the other's throat. Later, when the men had all gone, the Guv shot the other shifter in the head for embarrassing him in front of his friends. The last one…well, he was so broken down by everything that he just died—I think he gave up hoping."

My heart ached for the poor boy in my arms, but as he unburdened his soul he seemed to find some strength. He straightened up and looked directly at Luke. "I cleaned up the blood and buried the bodies. I can show the police where they are—that's more evidence against the Guv, isn't it?"

Luke smiled. "He won't know what hit him. Tell me, how did you get away?"

"There was a huge panic when you escaped," Milo answered, and I heard some amusement enter his voice. "They were so focused on getting the hell out of there before the police came that they forgot to even notice me."

"More fool them," Luke said with a grin, and Milo laughed softly.

I let go of Milo and pushed to my feet, knees complaining of their time on the hard floor. "Luke, why don't we go and see if the doctor is ready to discharge Milo, then he can come back with us today. Would that be alright with you, Milo?"

He nodded briskly and tossed the book onto the bed. "Yes, I'd like to leave here. The nurses have been lovely, but I feel like everyone's staring at me all the time."

"We'll be right back, then," Luke said, patting Milo's knee and getting up.

Outside, we passed Andy chatting with his colleagues, and made our way to the nurses' desk.

"Tell me something awful about you," I demanded of Luke while we waited to speak to someone.

His eyebrows rose in surprise and he barked a short laugh. "What on earth?"

I swallowed my own laughter. "You're perfect, too perfect. If you don't tell me something unsavoury about yourself then I'll think you're too good to be true."

Smiling until his cheek dimpled, he seemed to think for a second. "I often wake up with a puddle of drool on my pillow."

I snickered. "More."

"Well... I once farted so loudly that I woke myself up." He grinned.

My stomach cramped with suppressed laughter, and I gestured for him to go on.

"No," he declared. "No more or I'll be chasing you off."

I took a step closer to him and bumped my hip against his. "It will take more than a few misfiring bodily functions to chase me off."

The warmth of his smile and the heat in his gaze made me flush with pleasure. "Glad to hear it," he said in a low voice, and brushed his hand against mine.

Chapter Fourteen

Milo was eager to fill the gaps in his knowledge of werekind. After years of being rejected by one foster family after another when they found out he was a werewolf, and being made to feel like a freak, he had suppressed his abilities more effectively than any drug could. For several hours that evening he sat with us, listening with rapt attention while Luke spoke of things like silver and wolf's-bane, and the effects of the moon's cycle on individual werewolves, depending on which phase they were born within. They worked out that Milo was born under a crescent moon, and would therefore be more susceptible to the moon's influence at that time every month, but because he, like Luke, had been born a werewolf, the moon, with all her power, did not hold sway over them.

"That doesn't mean we were born with infinite control, however, like everything else it has to be learned. Some shifters never take on human form, while others choose never to assume animal form. Most are like me. I made the decision to embrace both halves of my soul, but just making the decision wasn't enough." Luke added a log to the fire in the living room and leant back against the sofa upon which I was seated. His head was so close to me that I couldn't resist the desire to run my fingers through the glossy strands of his blond hair. He rubbed his head against my hand, and I lightly scratched at his scalp. "There's a wildness in us, Milo, an atom, at our very core, a legacy from the original ones. I've worked hard to master that wildness, to find balance, so that, no matter how strong she may be, I won't be a slave to the call of Luna."

"Luna—the moon," Milo said, voice shaded with something like awe. "Will...will you teach me? Help me learn?"

"It would be my honour, but not this evening," Luke replied. "Our detective friends will be here soon to discuss the security measures they'll be taking. Speaking of which..." He pointed back over his shoulder a split second before the intercom buzzed.

Milo grinned. "I totally want to learn how to do that."

* * * *

"Armed bodyguards and round the clock patrols—when did life become a bad action movie?" I asked two hours later. Milo, fading fast, had been dispatched to the guest room, and the gates had closed on Ken and his team.

Luke came up behind me where I stood on the back patio, and wrapped his arms around me. I was instantly warmer, and when he nuzzled my neck I sighed in contentment.

"Ken promised we won't see more of them than the occasional shadow," he whispered, breath hot against my skin.

"But you'll know they're there, won't you? Even when we can't see them." What must it be like, I wondered, to see and hear things, to *sense* things no man ever could? He must have thought my question rhetorical, because he gave no answer, but instead continued his oral trip along my neck. I shivered with need, and my eyelids felt weighted.

He eased his hand down the front of my jeans and I gasped, pushing my hips forward until his fingers grazed my rapidly burgeoning cock. He mirrored my movement so that I could feel his own hardness press into the small of my back. "I want you," he moaned.

"God, yes." I let my head fall back against his shoulder, and through the slits of my eyes I saw the moon, hanging full and heavy in a midnight blue sky. "The moon's full."

"Do you want me to howl for you?" he asked, clearly amused.

"No, you might wake Milo, and I'd rather not have an audience when I'm riding your cock."

A shudder ran through Luke's big body, and he tightened his hand convulsively on my dick. Pleasure shot straight to my balls and I whimpered.

"Come with me," he said, voice low-pitched and rough. He withdrew his hand from my jeans, linked his fingers with mine and tugged me in the direction of his studio. He didn't turn on the lights, but guided me by the glow of the moon to a long work bench, spun me around and pushed me none too gently back against it. There was fire in his ice blue eyes, and he pulled impatiently at the fastenings of my jeans.

"Oh, fuck, Luke, *hurry.*" I was already grinding my crotch against his thigh in search of friction, nearly blind with need and breathing like I'd run a race.

He tore at my clothing until my jeans and underwear were around my thighs, then did the same with his own, before pulling me in and sealing our mouths together in a frantic kiss that was all teeth and tongues and desperation.

"Turn around," he ordered, and I immediately complied, gripping the edge of the bench and pushing my arse out.

Luke fumbled around for a moment, cursing, then, just as a foreign smell reached my nose, I felt his fingers circling my hole, massaging in something cool and viscous. I tried to open my legs farther, but was hampered by my jeans and muttered my own curse.

"Eager, baby?" he asked, just a hint of teasing in his voice. He pressed a couple of fingers deep into me and I rose onto my toes with a whine.

"Oh, do it, Luke, please. Do it now. *Now,*" I begged, nails digging into the work surface. I was wound so tight that I felt like I might snap at any second.

Teasing apparently forgotten, he plunged into me, balls deep on the first stroke. I cried out in wordless jubilation and locked my knees when he started to thrust.

"Oh, fuck, Hal," Luke exclaimed, fingers digging into my hips. "My Hal... So fucking *good.*"

The studio echoed with our pleasure — broken off sentences and choked cries. I was building fast towards release, but when Luke reached around and took me in hand I pitched over the edge, body jerking, breath stuttering in my chest. He followed soon after with a rapid snapping of hips and a long groan.

I slumped over the work bench, fighting to draw air into my lungs, a task made no easier with the weight of Luke draped over my back. It was freezing outside, but we were generating enough heat to fog up the windows.

"I fucking love the full moon," I said when I was finally able to string a coherent thought together.

Luke's body shook with silent laughter and he dropped a trail of kisses along my hairline. I grumbled my discontent when he moved, but allowed him to put my clothing back in order without offering any help or resistance.

"I have something for you," he said, and I turned around to find that he too was once again respectably dressed. He switched on a single overhead light, then opened a drawer in the work bench and took out something wrapped in black cloth. "I found the stone years ago, and knew that I would give it to my mate."

While he was still holding it, I peeled back the cloth to reveal a small, silvery-white stone attached to a thin leather cord. I picked it up and held it up to the light. It seemed to glow and shimmer. "It's beautiful, Luke. What is it?"

"It's a moonstone," he said and, taking it from me, he fastened it around my neck. The stone nestled comfortably in the hollow of my throat, and soon warmed against my skin. "It will keep you safe and bring you good fortune."

I had to swallow past a lump of emotion before I could speak. "It... It feels right," I said, running my fingers over its smooth contours.

"The most important thing about it," Luke said, taking my hand and lifting it to his mouth where he brushed his lips over my knuckles in an achingly tender gesture. "Is that when one lover gives it to another under a full moon, it means they will always have passion between them."

"I think I might actually cry now," I said, and sure enough, my eyes began to burn.

He smiled and added kisses to my fingertips. "If I have my way, Hal, you will only ever cry tears of happiness."

* * * *

The cavalry arrived at six the next morning—a small army of serious-faced men checking out the perimeter of the property, accompanied by a team of technicians who proceeded to investigate every circuit and chip of the security system. While Luke dealt with the supervising officer, I ushered a concerned-looking Milo into the kitchen to help me with breakfast.

I put sausages and bacon into the grill and Milo mixed up some scrambled eggs.

"Do you think we should make some tea and coffee for the policemen?" Milo asked shyly, as if expecting his suggestion to be laughed down. "It's still really early, and it looks freezing outside."

I smiled and nodded. "I think that's a great idea. Why don't you see if there are any flasks in the pantry, and I'll put on some extra sausages and bacon?"

Blushing, he ducked his head, but not before I saw his pleased smile. The poor kid was so lacking in confidence, I wondered if he'd ever received any praise in his life.

Half an hour later, the hall table held a tray of breakfast sandwiches, flasks of tea and coffee, every spare mug we could find, milk, sugar, and a pile of kitchen towel napkins.

When Luke, Milo and I went to the kitchen to have our own morning meal, we left behind us a considerably friendlier protection unit.

"I'm going to contact the agent about this house, today," Luke said over his second cup of coffee. "I want to put in an offer to buy."

"You think the owners will sell?" I asked.

Luke nodded. "I think so, they only rented because the arse was falling out of the market and they couldn't get the price they were looking for. I need to try to get some work done, too."

"I have a pile of emails to get through," I said, reaching for another slice of toast. "What about you, Milo?"

"I thought I might..." He pushed his food around his plate for a moment, then glanced up at Luke from under the cover of his hair. "Uh, I saw an X-Box in the living room..."

Luke smiled warmly at the boy, and I saw Milo's posture relax. "Help yourself, you'll find plenty of games in the cupboard to the right of the TV stand. But later, we'll start our lessons, okay?"

"I'd like that," Milo replied, unable to disguise his excitement.

We cleared away the breakfast things between us, and when Milo headed for the living room, I set up my laptop at the kitchen table where I had a good view of the garden and Luke's studio, but could also hear the electronic noises of Milo's games.

"Come and see me when you've finished your business," Luke said, bending to catch my mouth in a heated, but too-brief kiss.

Promising that I would, I watched him leave through the patio doors and cross the frosty lawn to his studio. He was wearing old jeans and a black T-shirt that clung perfectly to his lean torso. Just looking at him was enough to send a tingle along my spine. But there was another sensation niggling at my gut, something much less pleasant.

I looked at the small clock in the bottom corner of my laptop screen. It was just after seven. Had the raid on Doubleday's properties taken place, already? The sun was just starting to rise, and Ken had mentioned dawn. Were they just now knocking on—or *down*—his doors? What would they find, I wondered? What if they found nothing and decided they didn't have enough evidence to go to trial? Concern for the safety of Luke and Milo cramped my stomach, and I began to regret having such a big breakfast.

Determinedly, I tried to push the negative thoughts from my mind and opened my email account. I scanned the inbox, deciding which needed my immediate attention, which could wait, and which could be deleted unopened. Several of the emails were from my agent. I made a mental note to contact him, then went online to place a large grocery order for delivery—Luke's kitchen was well-stocked, but we would likely be holed up there for a while, with several extra mouths to feed.

I managed to concentrate enough to work steadily for a while, pausing to refill my coffee mug, and see off the tech team when they'd finished, leaving just the three of us in the house again.

The whole time, however, I was never quite able to shed the nervous flutter in my stomach, and found my attention drifting between the hazy image of Luke moving around in the studio, the sounds of Milo in the living room, and the clock on the wall, waiting for the phone to ring or a buzz from the intercom. When it came, would it be good news or bad?

When the patio door opened, admitting a blast of cold air, I was so lost in thought that I nearly jumped out of my skin.

"Anxiety is pouring off you in waves, love," Luke said, coming into the room and crouching beside my chair. He draped one arm over my lap, and curled his other hand around the back of my neck. "I'm sure I would have felt it even without werewolf senses."

It was odd that the simple fact of his presence was enough to quell most of my disquiet. I sighed and lifted my hand to his face, tracing the line of his eyebrows with my thumb. "You've become so important to me, so fast. How is that even possible?"

He smiled and touched his lips to mine. His kiss tasted like comfort. "Our fates are decided by powers far greater than us, my Hal."

"I can't help feeling like I'm waiting for the other shoe to drop," I said, a whispered confession.

"I won't accept that we've been brought together only to be torn apart so soon," Luke retorted, a light of certainty glinting in his eye. "Our story is just beginning."

I wanted, more than anything, to believe him.

"I want to start Milo's training, will you come with me?" he asked, getting to his feet and holding his hand out for mine. I nodded, closed my fingers around his and let him pull me up and lead me out of the kitchen.

* * * *

"I can't do it," Milo exclaimed, spinning away from Luke with a frustrated sigh. "I'm rubbish."

"You're not rubbish, Milo," Luke returned patiently. "This is a big deal, and we've only been working for a couple of hours—you're not going to learn everything today."

"I can't even shift," Milo bit out. "How is *breathing* going to help that?"

Luke turned the boy to face him and put his hands on Milo's shoulders. "It's not just breathing—you're learning to tune out your surroundings and focus on yourself."

"Sounds like dippy hippy shit to me." Milo pouted, and I saw Luke fight a smile.

"Maybe so, but you've buried the wolf deep, and you're living on the surface. If you want to reconnect with the other half of yourself you're going to have to embrace your inner hippy."

I couldn't help the laughter that burst from me, but the light of amusement shimmered in Milo's eyes too. I was lying on one of the sofas, feeling quite a bit more relaxed than I had earlier—the meditation exercises might not have been to Milo's taste, but even just observing had done me a power of good.

"We'll take a break for now," Luke said. "But believe it or not, you are actually making progress. For the first time, I sensed your wolf stir from his slumber."

Milo's eyes widened, and he sucked in a surprised breath. "Seriously?"

"Most definitely." Luke smiled. "Why don't we have some food and try again this afternoon?"

Milo nodded with renewed enthusiasm, and there was a bounce in his step when he left the room.

"You may have to carry me," I said to Luke. "My inner hippy is too mellowed out to move."

Luke grinned, took my hands and pulled me to my feet. "Should I throw you over my shoulder like a fireman?"

"Ooh, role play. I like!"

That elicited a sound from Luke that was half-laugh, half-growl, and he dragged me into a crushing embrace. "I don't suppose we can send the kid out to the movies?"

I snickered and reached around to grab his arse. "Looks like Milo isn't the only one who needs to learn a little control."

"There are some circumstances in which control is not only over-rated, but unforgivable," he claimed, and lowered his head to the crook of my neck.

I laughed breathlessly, letting my head fall back. "I can't believe you said that with a straight face."

"You're intoxicating," he said roughly. "I can't get enough."

The concept of resistance had been foreign to me since meeting Luke and, had it not been for the knock on the front door, I have no doubt that I would have succumbed to the heat we seemed to generate between us, just by touching.

Sighing, Luke dropped his forehead to rest on my shoulder. I stroked my hand over his hair and laughed softly.

"Hold that thought, baby," I said. I eased out of his arms with no little reluctance, and headed for the front door, but Luke was faster, placing himself between me and whoever was calling on us. When he opened the door I saw that it was Ken and his 'specialised unit' team. My breath got caught in my throat, and without realising it I was clutching at Luke's arm.

A slow smile broke out on Ken's face, and the light of triumph glinted in his eyes. "We got him," he said, simply, and relief made me lightheaded.

Chapter Fifteen

"You have him in custody?" Luke asked, gesturing for the officers to enter. Once inside, he led the way through to the kitchen, where Milo was setting three places at the table for lunch.

Ken smiled and took a seat at the island. "He's sweating in a cell as we speak."

Following their boss' lead, Matt and Andy sat too, but Georgie remained standing at the far end of the island, fidgeting with her leather folio and casting occasional glances in Luke's direction. She looked nervous, and I recalled the way Luke had turned on her in the interview room. Was it possible that she was frightened of him?

"The search went well, then?" Luke asked, apparently oblivious to the looks he was getting from Ken's second in command.

"I'd say we pretty much hit the jackpot." Ken grinned.

"What did you find?" I asked, professional curiosity piqued.

"A laptop," Ken said. "The files on it contained lists of the people who paid to attend the fights, records of bets made, payments made to a doctor for the purchase of barbiturates and Rohypnol, and a known arms dealer for stun guns and a Smith & Wesson revolver. Financial records also showed transactions with a South African gunsmith for a special order of silver bullets. The Prime Order files were there too — names and addresses of every known shifter in the country. Apparently Robert Doubleday used the files to track down werewolves with no pack to offer them any kind of protection."

I sank down onto a stool and reached for Luke's hand. "Jesus. And this was in his *home*?"

Ken shook his head. "Doubleday owns over a dozen commercial properties in Greater London. An analysis of his car's GPS system showed that he only visited one with any regularity, so we focused the search between there and his home. We found the laptop there, in a floor safe, along with the revolver. The files were encrypted, of course. The security was good, but our tech guy is better. We can also place him at Humblebee Farm, thanks to his fingerprints on the nicotine gum packet."

"We found a mobile phone at the house," Matt added. "The call history showed communications with the doctor, the arms dealer, and every client on the spectator list. It was unregistered, but Doubleday's prints were all over that too."

"Jason, the tech guy, is already working on the financials and phone records of the doctor and the arms dealer," Andy said. "If we can make a solid connection between them and Doubleday, we can cut a deal with them to point the finger at Doubleday."

"Sounds like a good day's work," Luke said. "His lawyers can't possibly pick all that apart."

"Your testimony, and that of young Milo, is still our best evidence, of course," Ken said pointedly.

Luke nodded. "Understood, right, Milo?"

While the conversation had been going on the boy had been nervously fiddling with the coffee maker. He turned at the sound of Luke's voice, and nodded jerkily.

"Detective Trask, uh…" Milo coughed to clear his throat before approaching the island. "About the gun…"

"Ah." Ken looked momentarily disappointed. "The most we can get him with there is illegal possession of a firearm. There doesn't seem to be a direct connection to this crime."

Milo glanced at Luke, then back at Ken. "I-I can give you one." He proceeded to tell the officers about the other shifters at the farm, and how he'd personally witnessed Doubleday shoot one of the shifters. "I can show you where they're buried."

For a second, Ken looked stunned, then he turned to Georgie and pointed at the folio she'd been holding in front of her like a shield. "Have you got that map of the farm in there?"

Unzipping the case, she took out a paper document that had been folded several times. She handed it to Ken who spread it out on the island.

"Can you show me on the map, Milo?"

Milo's hand shook as he pointed to the area behind the stable block. "The, uh, the graves aren't very deep, and there's a big old tree right beside them—I carved my initials in the tree so that I would be able to find it again, if I had to."

"Excellent job, Milo," Luke praised, and the boy flushed and smiled.

Ken nodded his emphatic agreement, and turned to his colleagues. "Right, looks like we have more work to do." Matt and Andy grumbled but I didn't hear any real dissent in their tones. Georgie put the map back in her folder and was first to head for the door.

I followed her out into the hall. "He wouldn't really have hurt you, you know, he was just in a very…vulnerable place, and he was protecting his territory, I guess."

She blushed with embarrassment and looked at the toes of her shoes. "I wouldn't have come here if I thought differently, but, well, I don't mind admitting that it scared the crap out of me. I'll get over it," she added with a smile.

"I hope so—wolf or man, he's the most decent person I've ever met."

Her smile deepened, and she nodded, opening the front door.

Feeling Luke's eyes on me, I turned to find him watching us, but rather than going all teeth and claws on Georgie, he simply winked at me.

"I need to have a word with the security supervisor before we leave," Ken said, crossing the hall to the door. "Any problems or concerns that you want to flag up?"

Luke shook his head. "Just tell them that if they see a big white dog in the garden, don't shoot."

"Heaven forefend," Ken laughed.

"Detective," I said before he could leave. "I need to go back to my own house for a while tomorrow—I wasn't planning for the long haul when I packed my overnight bag."

"I'll take you," Luke said immediately.

"No!" Ken and I spoke at exactly the same time.

"I'm afraid not, Luke," Ken continued. "It's too dangerous for both of you, you have to keep as low a profile as possible—can't have any paparazzi snapping a quick pic of you with Hal. I'll have a couple of my men accompany him."

I started at that. I'd almost forgotten all the crap that was going on back there.

Luke's eyes narrowed mutinously, but I laid a placating hand on his chest. "Just a quick trip to pick up some clean undies and some work files I need. I'll be there and back in a couple of hours."

"I can go with him," Andy offered. "You know, a familiar face."

"All right, but make sure you sign out a side arm, and take one of the protection guys with you," Ken said.

Andy nodded. "Will do, boss. I'll collect you at ten in the morning, okay?"

"That's great, thanks."

They left and I closed the door on the frozen air, then turned to see Luke watching me with a disgruntled expression, arms crossed over his wide chest so that the muscles of his biceps bulged, practically begging me to touch.

"If the plan was to make me shiver with fear at the big angry wolf," I said, moving slowly towards him. "You should try not to look so hot."

"I don't want you going without me," he stated, ignoring my words.

I sighed with feigned exasperation. "And I don't want to go in to lunch with a hard on, but sometimes we have to just play the cards we're dealt."

Rolling his eyes, Luke bit out a curse. "Stubborn man."

I laughed and turned him back towards the kitchen, appreciating the feel of all that power under my hands. "Oh, you have no idea."

* * * *

I stirred early the following morning. It was still dark outside, and the full moon — in the second day of its three day phase — cast an unearthly glow through the slats of the window blinds. Luke was wrapped around me, and if asked at that moment what kind of shifter my lover was, I would have had no hesitation in answering — octopus. My bladder was informing me of the urgent need to pee, but every time I wriggled out from the embrace of one of Luke's arms, another seemed to take its place. If I hadn't been afraid that I would wet the bed for the first time since I was a child, I would have found the situation amusing.

"Luke, you have to let me go, love,"

"No," he mumbled sleepily, and pulled me even closer. "Keep you safe…mine."

"Yes, yours," I agreed, trying once more to loosen the tight band of his arms around me. "But the only thing I'm in danger of right now is pissing myself."

Luke blinked a few times and opened bleary eyes. "Hmm, what?"

Laughing quietly, I pushed his tousled blond hair back from his face. "I need to go to the loo, baby, like *now*."

"Oh, okay," he said, and I was able to slip free. "Hurry back."

I glanced at him over my shoulder while I pulled on a pair of shorts. "Will you make it worth my while?"

Stretching sinuously, the sheet pooled around his narrow hips, he ran the tip of his tongue over the point of a fang. "I have something very special in mind for you."

Adrenaline spiked in my blood and weakened my knees. "Dear God, I don't know whether to be turned on or terrified."

Luke grinned, and I saw something of the wild in that smile. "I think I know," he said, dropping his gaze to where my dick was rising to push against the front of my shorts. I almost forgot the demands of my bladder.

Shaking my head, I walked on unsteady legs to the door. "Bad wolf!"

His soft laughter followed me across the hall to the bathroom. I relieved myself, washed my hands and brushed my teeth, and was just about to open the door when a low snarling growl reached my ears. Snickering, I pulled open the door just as Luke appeared in the doorway of the bedroom. Like me, he was wearing only his boxer shorts.

"Have you forgotten we have a teenager in the house?" I asked, leaning against the frame and cocking my hip in a way that I hoped looked seductive.

But instead of smiling, Luke frowned. "That wasn't me."

I straightened up just as the sound came again, from the direction of Milo's bedroom. "What...?"

Luke shrugged and crossed the hall, then laid his hand flat on Milo's door. He took a deep breath. "*Oh.*"

"Luke, what is it?" I asked, voice hushed with just an edge of panic.

Without answering, Luke pressed down on the handle and opened the door slowly. The growling noise came again, but rather than look worried, Luke smiled. It was as close to sappy as I'd seen him.

Intrigued, I stepped closer and stood on my toes to look over his shoulder. I immediately raised my hand to my mouth to muffle a gasp at the sight that greeted me. Milo — for it could only be Milo, with that tawny colouring and those big brown eyes — stood in the middle of the room, on *all fours*, pointed ears perked up in interest at our presence, and considerably more hirsute than he'd been when he went to bed the night before.

"Wonderful," Luke exclaimed, and between one breath and the next he too was shifting, smooth skin transforming into soft white fur, hands and feet curling into paws, nails thickening and becoming claws. Where there had been a human face was now a wolf's snout. But those eyes... The eyes I would recognise anywhere. He bumped my leg affectionately before turning and going to Milo.

He bared his teeth and seemed to square his shoulders. Milo dipped his head and sank to lie on the floor — submission to the Alpha. I held my breath as I waited for Luke's response. This was clearly a ritual that came naturally to them. Did it involve violence? Surely Luke the Alpha wouldn't be driven to hurt the boy to prove his dominance?

Luke moved closer to Milo, all power and grace, and nudged the young wolf's head with his own before stepping back again. Milo seemed to take this for acceptance, or approval, because he returned to a standing position, though his head remained slightly bowed.

With that, Luke shifted back to human form, retrieved his boxers and smiled widely as he slipped into them. Milo's shift back was less fluid, and took longer. For a worrying moment I thought he might get stuck between two forms, he seemed to be having such difficulty, and I clutched at Luke's arm, unable to speak but silently begging him to help. Luke simply squeezed my hand in reassurance.

When at last he achieved full human form, Milo lay on the floor, sweating and breathing heavily. He looked utterly exhausted, but when he raised his head to look at us, there was soul-deep pleasure in his expression.

"I did it," he whispered, pushing himself, with some effort, to sit up.

"Yes, you did," Luke replied, and there was genuine pride and respect in his voice. "How did you manage it?

Milo reached for the pyjama trousers he'd been sleeping in and struggled into them, then levered himself up off the floor to sit on the side of the bed. "I couldn't sleep, so I decided to try the hippy exercises again. I think it was easier on my own, when I wasn't, you know, trying to impress you." He shrugged and coloured, but there was a smile on his lips that nothing, I was certain, could have removed.

"Well," Luke said, reaching over to grab the boy's thin shoulder. "You can consider me thoroughly impressed. We should go for a run together."

Milo's eyes lit up. "Us? In the garden?"

"Better than that," Luke said with an impish grin. "Right behind the studio, hidden by a couple of trees, there's a small wooden door, and on the other side there's about fifty acres of unspoilt woodland."

Milo gasped. "That would be fucking awesome!"

"Not on your lives," I stated, moving farther into the room. "I hate to be a killjoy here, guys, but that is *not* happening. There are armed guards around this house for a reason, and I'm not about to allow you to put yourselves at risk for a jaunt in the woods. Nope. Not happening."

Luke snorted loudly, and leaned closer to me to press a kiss to my temple. "Whatever you say, dear."

"And here I thought you were the one in charge around here," Milo said to Luke, barely suppressing his own amusement.

I tossed him my best withering look, happy to see that it made not a jot of a difference to his smile, and glanced at the clock on his bedside table. Six-fourteen. "Milo, you look shattered, go back to bed and try to get some sleep. You" — I poked Luke in the shoulder — "come with me." I wanted to find out about the 'something special' he had promised.

* * * *

"Promise me that you and Milo won't sneak off alone for a quick run in the woods," I said as I prepared for the arrival of Andy to take me into London.

"Wolf scout's honour," Luke replied, touching three fingers to his forehead.

I narrowed my eyes and tilted my head. "Seriously?"

His eyes widened in puppy innocence. "What? That's a real thing."

Swallowing a laugh, I buttoned my coat and reached for my scarf. "Whatever you say. Just…try to be good."

"I always *try*," he retorted, grinning unabashedly. The smile faded, however, when we heard the car pull up into the driveway, and he took my face between his big hands and kissed me with melting tenderness. "A little down payment for later."

My skin heated and tightened, and I licked my lips to savour the taste of him. "I'll be back as soon as I can."

For a minute I thought he wasn't going to let me go, but he finally dropped his hands from my face and led the way to the front door.

Andy was out of the car and opening the boot when I stepped outside into the frigid air.

"Georgie asked me to bring the kid's things over." He took out a single duffle bag and a cardboard box. Milo's worldly possessions. My heart actually hurt.

Luke came forward to take them from him.

"Be good and I'll bring you back something nice," I teased, pecking Luke's cheek and getting into the back of the car. I could feel his eyes following me all the way down the driveway until the officer on duty closed the gates behind us.

Andy was at the wheel, and a burly looking officer rode silent shotgun beside him. About five minutes down the road we had to make way for a supermarket truck, and I suddenly remembered that I hadn't told Luke about the delivery. I dug my phone out of my pocket to send him a quick text as the truck passed us, noticing that there were two men in the cab. I didn't think the order I'd placed had been that big — I'd only ever been graced by one delivery man at my place.

The journey to my house in Fulham was nearly an hour long, so I made myself comfortable and watched the scenery pass. Winter had well and truly set in. The denuded trees shimmered with frost and a moist fog hung low over the roads. Even though I was in the warmth of the car, I pulled my scarf a little tighter around my neck.

The city seemed big and noisy after the relative peace of Luke's home, and when we were forced to stop for road works, I had to laugh. "Welcome back to London, gentlemen."

A bored looking man with a stop sign let one car at a time through, slowing us down considerably. I began to get concerned that I wouldn't get back to Luke as quickly as I'd promised. I had no doubt that he would be worried. Finally we were second in the queue, and the car in front of us was waved through, pushing us to the front. I sighed with relief, but the breath of the sigh was still warm on my lips when everything went to hell.

The guy with the stop sign tossed it aside, reached inside his high-vis jacket and withdrew something that looked frighteningly like a gun. Before Andy and our silent companion had a chance to react, two other men dressed as road workers had descended on the car, both carrying similar weapons.

I cried out in shock when the front windscreen suddenly exploded in a glittering shower of glass fragments. There were a couple of loud popping sounds, and the two officers in front of me slumped, held upright only by their seat belts.

"Jesus Christ. Andy...*Andy*?" Panic made my voice shrill. I lurched forwards to check on them, only to be sharply jerked back by my own seat belt. I fumbled to get it free and tried again, but before I got very far the door beside me was yanked open, I was hauled out of the car, and the muzzle of a gun was pushed, with bruising force, under my chin.

"Just do what you're told, okay? You don't need to die too." Before I could reply, I was dragged away from the car towards a white panelled van and pushed inside.

In the second before the doors slammed shut I got a look at Andy and the other officer in the front of the car. A small patch of red was visible on each man's shirt, directly over their hearts.

Chapter Sixteen

The other three men climbed into the van, one at the wheel and two with me in the back, and the van lurched forwards, sending me sprawling on the dusty floor. My captors managed to stay on their feet, having grabbed onto bars at the sides, near the roof. Obviously they were more used to that particular situation than I.

I scrambled to a sitting position, adrenaline pumping like super fuel through my veins. "Who the fuck are you?"

"Shut it," the one closest to me sneered. He was big and bulky, with a head as round and shiny as a bowling ball.

"You just shot two police officers — you have a shit storm coming your way."

"I said shut it, you little prick." The toe of his boot connected with my torso, and a sharp pain shot through my already bruised ribs.

I gritted my teeth against the cry that rose in my throat. "Who are you? What do you want with me?"

Baldy rolled his eyes and looked like he'd smelt something particularly nasty. "Are you mentally defective?" he demanded, clenching his fist and drawing his arm back. I refused to close my eyes, or blink as I focused on him, even as my insides twisted and coiled in preparation for the blow.

But before it landed, the other guy in the back—less bulky, but just as tall, with buzz-cut hair—grabbed Baldy's arm and shook his head. "Enough. The boss wants him alive and conscious."

"The boss?" I asked, interest piqued. "Who's that? Who are you working for?"

Nothing. I guess they weren't in a sharing mood.

"Come on, guys, I'm going to meet him soon enough, yeah? You might as well tell me now." I had to brace myself against the floor when the driver took a corner too fast, and winced at the renewed pain in my ribs.

Baldy grinned. "You think that hurts, you fucking perv? You got no clue what's coming to you."

My gut contracted with fear at the threat, but his words, heavy with hate, caught my attention. Perv? What the hell did that mean? I'd been called many less than pleasant things in my life—as a journalist, and a gay man, mostly, but *perv* seemed somehow incongruous in those circumstances.

"Perv? What the fuck are you taking about?" I demanded, voice surprisingly steady, all things considered.

Baldy's face twisted in obvious distaste. "That's what you are, innit? What else can you call a man who shags *beasts*?"

Beasts? My eyes widened as realisation dawned. "You're working for Doubleday, aren't you? Not Robert, because he's all snug in a police cell right now, but Victor — he's the boss. You're part of all that Prime Order bullshit."

Face colouring with obvious rage, Baldy leaned closer to me, grabbed a handful of my hair and viciously jerked my head back. Buzz-cut was reaching for him again, but Baldy shrugged him off. "I should rip your fucking head off with my bare hands, arsehole. You're nothing, but a traitor to your race." He twisted his hand in my hair, until I gasped at the pain, then he grinned maliciously at me.

Eyes watering, I forced myself to smile back at him. "But you won't, will you? Because you're not allowed. You're not the boss, you're just a low-rent bitch who does his bidding."

He let go of my hair only to back-hand my face. My head snapped sharply to the side, and for a second it felt like my cheekbone might explode. "There's only one *bitch* around here," he retorted, spitting in his anger.

Even though my face ached with the effort, I continued to smile at him. "So, you know that my lover is a werewolf. Shall I tell you what you don't know? He's more man that you will ever be. He's an Alpha — he takes orders from no one, and he's certainly no one's glorified errand boy."

With a wordless cry of indignation, Baldy grabbed me by the throat and squeezed, blunt nails digging into my skin. I wrapped my hands around his wrist, but he would not be dislodged, until Buzz-cut shoved him forcefully enough that Baldy landed on his arse at the other side of the van.

"Jesus Christ, man," Buzz-cut muttered, looking down at his cohort. "Are you fucking trying to get yourself killed?"

"Oh, he'll die alright," I claimed, defiantly, clutching at my throat. "When my wolf comes for me—and he *will* come—he'll tear you apart for daring to lay a finger on me." I knew it was all bluff, of course. *I* had no idea who they were or where I was going, how could Luke possibly be expected to find me?

Shaking his head, Buzz-cut reached into a bag and took out a roll of gaffer tape. I knew it was for me, but couldn't resist another dig at the man sitting across from me, virtually foaming at the mouth. "This is a hair thing, isn't it? You hate wolves because they have so much hair and you have none. I bet if you got a pimple on your head it would look like a giant tit."

Buzz-cut tore a strip off the roll and pinched my face in one massive hand. "Have your fun now, boy, because I can promise you won't be doing much laughing later." He spoke quietly as he slapped the tape over my mouth, and there was a dark coldness in his eyes that seemed to suck all the warmth out of the air. Fear sliced through me, and I put up no resistance when he tore off more tape and used it to bind my wrists.

I ignored the snickering coming from Baldy, and rested my head back against the side of the van. From my position on the floor, all I could see out of the windows was the dull grey sky. After a while I closed my eyes and concentrated on Luke.

Can you hear me, love? Can you feel me? I'm in a bit of a pickle and I could really use your help.

He'd told me that he could read my thoughts, and I'd witnessed it several times. But at those times I'd been standing right next to him. Could it work at such a distance? More importantly, did I want it to? If Luke came after me he would be walking right into enemy hands. Just the thought made panic and nausea roil in my stomach.

I estimated we'd been on the move for about thirty minutes when the van slowed and idled for a minute, and I heard a whining and metallic scraping sound that suggested automated gates to me. The driver pulled forwards again, and stopped completely soon after. Guessing that we'd reached our destination, I breathed deeply through my nose in an attempt to dispel the heaving sensation in my gut. My heart was hammering against my ribs, and my pulse was racing so fast that I was beginning to feel lightheaded.

Reaching into his bag again, Buzz-cut this time withdrew a black hood and moved to put it over my head, but I instinctively dodged out of his reach. His obsidian eyes narrowed threateningly. "You can put this on or I can make you put it on. You don't want to test me, boy."

No, I really didn't. While Baldy was all naked fury and hair trigger, this guy was pure control. His voice never rose in pitch, his expression never changed, and his eyes held no emotion — not even anger. He was the kind of terrifying that Baldy could only ever aspire to be.

I was dragged from the van, and hustled blindly across a patch of gravel to a set of shallow stone steps, then inside, if the rise in temperature was anything to go by. The ground under my feet was smoother now, like marble or tile. I stumbled a couple of times, disoriented, but didn't fall, thanks to the hands clamped around my biceps. The temperature went up another degree or two, the air slightly humid now. With the smell of chlorine in my nostrils, and the rougher, non-slip texture of the flooring, it didn't take genius to figure out that I'd been brought to a swimming pool.

Holy fuck, they're going to drown me.

There was silence as my arms were pulled up over my head, and something new was secured around my wrists. The hood was removed then, and I automatically looked up. I'd been strung up like an animal carcass to a beam overhead. I glanced around at my surroundings, and guessed that I was in a private home, in a pool house surrounded on three sides by windows — a secluded location, then.

"Good morning, Mr Paxton," said a man I immediately recognised from old newspaper reports as Victor Doubleday. He stepped up to me and ripped the taped from my mouth.

I snorted, part amusement, mostly hysteria. "You sound like a Bond villain. Do you expect me to die?"

"Actually, I do," he replied, a small smile playing around his lips. I knew him to be in his late sixties, but he was still a good-looking man, with a military straight posture and steel-grey hair. "But only after you've served your purpose."

"Which would be?" I asked, testing the integrity of the rope securing my hands. Whoever had tied me up knew their knots.

"To bring the beast to me, of course," Doubleday answered, tucking his hands into the pockets of his trousers.

"You think he'll come for me?" I asked, deciding to ignore the beast comment. "You think he'll walk into a trap, for *me*?"

"I know he will. These creatures are driven by primeval urges," he said, lip curling with obvious disgust. "You are his mate, are you not? He'll have to come for you—intelligent thought doesn't play a part in their choices."

Some of my fear made way for annoyance. "You're still hanging on to all that *lesser being* bullshit, aren't you?"

His mouth tightened into a thin white line, and his nostrils flared. "Have you read your bible, Mr Paxton? God did not create shape-shifters of any kind. They are an abomination spawned by the enemies of all things good and true."

I'd heard it all before, of course, back when I'd been marching at uni, and Victor Doubleday's minions had been preaching his word. It didn't sound any less fucked up now than it had then.

Baldy and the driver were standing near the door, matching smirks on their equally ugly faces. Buzz-cut had his back to me, and was once again doing something with his bag. Doubleday turned to Baldy and the driver and nodded. "You know what to do." They both looked a little disappointed, but left without a word.

When Buzz-cut turned around I saw that he'd been using the gaffer tape again, this time to bind his own hands at the knuckles. I swallowed around the panic rising in my throat, and drew in a shuddering breath. Every muscle in my body seemed to spasm when he moved close enough to touch me, but I was surprised when he only reached inside my coat, took out my phone, and handed it to Doubleday.

The old man frowned and pushed a few buttons, then raised his head and directed a barely perceptible nod at Buzz-cut. The first punch caught me right in the solar plexus, and seemed to drive every breath of air from my lungs. I would have doubled up, both in reaction to the punch and in an attempt to protect myself, but, incapacitated as I was, I could only hang there and take every blow that Buzz-cut sent my way—I was a human punching bag.

I felt a couple of ribs collapse under the power of his fist, and tried to breathe my way through the dull pain—nothing sharp, so I chose to believe that meant there were no serious internal injuries. The taste of my own blood came as a shock, until I realised that he had moved from my torso to my face.

This was not the kind of pain I could breathe through—if I hadn't been hanging from a beam I wouldn't even have been able to stand. I closed my eyes as the blows rained down, splitting my lips, smashing into my jaw, chin and eye sockets. Everything ached, the kind of agony that begged for the bliss of unconsciousness.

Buzz-cut wasn't even out of breath.

I'm sure I let out a sob of thanks when Doubleday finally said, "That will be all for now." As if he was dismissing the butler.

Nodding, my assailant simply unwound the tape from his hand, put his jacket back on, and left. It was only then that I realised Doubleday had been videoing the beating on my phone.

I gagged on a mouthful of blood, and spat it onto the floor. With every second that passed my head felt like it was closer and closer to exploding. My vision began to swim, and my ears were ringing. Every time I tried to draw in a deep breath my broken ribs shifted and I was racked with agony.

"It gives me no pleasure to see a fellow human being suffer like this, Mr Paxton," Doubleday said, putting my phone down on a glass-topped table. "Even one who has made such deplorable choices in his life."

I couldn't seem to focus on his face, or summon the energy to be angry at his words. My legs started to weaken and give out under me until I was taking the full weight of my body in my wrists. The smell of chlorine was still strong, and I thought of the pool I'd learnt to swim in as a boy... Mum had insisted I wear those little water wing things on my arms... We'd gone for tea and cake after. The smell of chlorine always made me think of lemon drizzle cake. Or was it ginger cake? I couldn't seem to remember...

* * * *

"Hal? Come on, Hal, wake up."

"Hmm...?" I came round slowly to the feel of someone tapping on my cheek. I felt hungover, thick-headed and dizzy. My head was throbbing...no, not just my head...everything hurt. What...? I tried to open my eyes, but they felt sore and swollen, and I only managed to open one part way. When I was able to focus and saw Andy Webster, everything came rushing back with enough force to cause actual pain in my battered head. I was suddenly overwhelmed with sadness. "Am I dead too?"

He laughed softly. "No, Hal, you're not dead. Not yet." The smile twisted into a sneer, and my head snapped to the side when he backhanded me just as Baldy had in the van, and on the same fucking cheekbone.

"What's going on?" My lips were sticky with congealed blood, and my head felt heavy when I moved it. Andy was standing next to Victor Doubleday, and I couldn't begin to figure things out in my fuzzy mind.

"Why don't we cut Mr Paxton down from there?" Doubleday asked pleasantly. "He looks like he could use a seat."

Andy dragged a chair over from the table and positioned it behind me. He then reached into his jacket, withdrew a knife, and cut the rope that had been holding me up. I slumped into the chair, gasping in shock at the pain that radiated out from my ribs.

"I-I don't understand," I said breathlessly. "How are you alive? I saw…"

"Tranquiliser dart," Andy explained, touching his chest. "Just a mild sedative to make it look real. Left a bloody hole in my favourite shirt, though."

"But…why?" God, I couldn't think straight. Nothing was making sense, and everything hurt so fucking much.

"It seems that Andy and I have a common problem," Doubleday said. "We both have loved ones languishing at Her Majesty's pleasure because of you and your…lover."

My expression must have revealed my continued incomprehension, because Andy moved to crouch in front of me. "John Stoke," he said simply.

I frowned—and even that hurt. "The *Farmer*?"

"My stepfather," Andy corrected coldly. "A good man, and one of the best cops the Met ever had."

I shook my head. "No, that's not…he was corrupt. He sent innocent men to prison and let guilty men go free, for *money*."

"Lies," Andy exclaimed, springing to his feet. "You took the word of a career criminal and ruined a great man."

"There was…*is* evidence," I argued, pushing through the fog of pain to concentrate. "I didn't write a word that wasn't true."

"*Shut up*," he demanded, eyes dark with loathing for me. "Because of your *lies* my life has been shattered. The man who raised me like his own son is rotting in a prison—do you know what happens to former cops in prison? My mother is a wreck—she can't even look after herself anymore. I've had to put her in a nursing home, but not a nice private one, no, we can't afford that since all Dad's money and assets were frozen. She's in a shithole local authority place. The only reason I still have a job is because I kept my own name instead of taking his."

"I'm sorry," I said quietly. "I'm sorry you and your mum have been hurt, but I told the truth."

"You fucking journalists wouldn't know the truth if it bit you on the arse," he seethed. "Everybody knows that you make up all that shit in the papers. Now you're making a small fortune off the back of my family's misery."

There would be no reasoning with him—that much was obvious. But I still couldn't get my befuddled brain around the situation. "I still don't understand...*this*." I gestured around me. My wrists were still bound with tape, and my hands tingled as the blood started to return to them.

"I want my son freed, Mr Paxton," Doubleday said, in that eerily polite way he had. "That creature you're bedding is the biggest barrier to that. If he is unable to testify—and by extension, the boy, because we both know he won't have the courage to stand up alone—then my barristers will be able to argue that all evidence that sprang from his police statement should be inadmissible in court. But with the protection around them I found I was unable to get near him. I was beginning to despair when this young man came to me with a deal."

"Let me guess," I said, as the pieces began to fall into place. "Supercop here brings you *me*. You use me to draw out Luke, and you kill us both. He gets his revenge and sonny-boy goes free."

Doubleday smiled. "Concise and to the point. I can see why you were a successful reporter."

"The big flaw in the plan being that you are both fucking insane." I tried to laugh, but my ribs protested and it came out as more of a groan.

"Name calling? A little beneath your talents, isn't it, Mr Paxton?" In spite of his mild tone, anger flickered in Doubleday's eyes. He turned back to the table and picked up a small leather case, then opened it and took out a full syringe. "Do you know what this is? No, of course you don't. It's a substance called colloidal silver — nano-particles of silver suspended in liquid. A little gift for your lover."

Silver? Oh, that couldn't be good.

"I see from your expression that you have an inkling of what this could mean," he continued, smiling coldly and turning the syringe in his hands. "It won't kill him, but it will cause him such excruciating agonies that he will beg for death."

"The gun?" I asked, nodding to the weapon I could see now that the leather case had been moved.

Doubleday smiled and shrugged. "Silver bullets — just in case."

My blood ran cold at the pleasure he seemed to take from the idea. *Stay away, Luke, stay away from this place.*

"You can't think you'll just walk away from this," I said to Andy. "Maybe they'll put you in the same prison as your old man."

Andy laughed, a spiky, bitter sound. "They sent me home to rest — as far as anyone outside this room is concerned, I'm at home, all tucked up in bed."

"Quite the hero," Doubleday joked.

A noise from the room next door caught my attention, and I turned to see the men from the van coming back, but this time they had company. Luke was with them, one man on either side of him and one behind.

At the same time as our eyes met, I felt the cold steel of Andy's knife press against my throat.

Chapter Seventeen

Luke's hands were clenched into white-knuckled fists at his sides, and rage blazed in his eyes. "They'll pay dearly for every bruise inflicted and every drop of blood spilled," he promised me, and I felt the certainty of it in my soul.

But right at that moment, my own situation was the least of my worries. My eyes flicked to the syringe in Doubleday's hand. Luke's gaze followed, and I prayed he would understand that my concerns lay with him. He nodded imperceptibly, and I felt a flicker of relief, but it was like spitting on a bonfire—not nearly enough to conquer the alarm stampeding wildly through my veins.

"Andy, I'm very sorry to see you here," Luke said with remarkable calm.

"You don't seem surprised though." There was a tremor of uncertainty in the detective's voice, and the pressure of the blade at my throat lessened somewhat.

Luke smiled, but there was nothing friendly in it. "I smelt you before I even walked through the front door. You reek of fear."

"What have I got to be afraid of?" Andy challenged, pressing the blade close again, however, his hand didn't seem quite as steady as before. "I'm not the one with the knife at my throat."

"Yes, about that," Luke replied. "If you remove it now I might let you live."

Doubleday laughed at that. "You're really rather amusing. In different circumstances I might consider keeping you as a pet. I wonder, do you shed hair on the furniture like a dog?"

Only a slight tick in his clenched jaw revealed Luke's anger. "I kept my end of the deal, now you do the same."

"You told no one? No police?" Doubleday asked, still turning the syringe in his hands.

"You know I didn't," Luke bit out. "Your text message was very specific, and even if I had, your thugs had me change cars so many times and took such a circuitous route that no one could have followed. You've got me. Now, let Hal go."

"What? *No.*" Shock and disbelief seized me. Luke was exchanging his life for mine?

"What the hell are you talking about?" Andy demanded. He gestured between himself and Doubleday. "*We* had a deal—you get the werewolf, and I get Paxton."

Doubleday smiled benevolently. "Calm down, Detective. The beast knows I have no intention of letting Mr Paxton go, don't you? It would defeat the whole purpose of the exercise, after all."

"I had assumed as much," Luke admitted. "But I thought I would give you the chance to act like the gentleman you pretend to be." With a swiftness and efficiency that took my breath away, Luke dealt with his three man escort—his fists came up and back, smashing into the faces of the two flanking him, and a split second later he snapped his head back so that it connected with the head of the man behind him.

They clutched at their faces, moaning in pain, and fell forwards. Before their knees had even hit the tile floor, Luke had shifted and was leaping towards Doubleday. The man seemed to be transfixed by the exhibition of skill and grace, and it was easy for Luke to knock the syringe from his limp fingers. It fell to the floor and rolled into the pool, barely making a sound.

Luke roared and took Doubleday down then, great paws on the man's chest, teeth bared, and snarling just an inch from Doubleday's suddenly chalk-white face.

Apparently equally enthralled by what he was seeing, Andy had let the knife slip from my throat to rest on my shoulder, so when I saw Baldy drag himself up from the floor, blood pouring from his nose, to the table where he wrapped his fingers around the gun, I took the opportunity to slip from the chair onto the floor. My ribs screamed in agony, but when he took aim in Luke's direction, I lunged across the floor and lashed out with my feet, sweeping his legs out from under him again.

He managed to retain his grip on the gun, however, and, in spite of landing on his back with enough force to drive the air from his lungs in a loud *whoosh*, he was able to squeeze the trigger. The bang echoed around the cavernous room. I started, but my blood froze when I heard a high-pitched yelp. My head snapped around just in time to see Luke, still in wolf form, jerk away from Doubleday, and tumble into the pool. A red cloud immediately bloomed around him.

Fear ripped through me, and I scrambled towards him, hands still bound, body vehemently protesting every inch gained. Tears of panic blurred my vision.

Luke was sinking to the bottom of the pool, leaving a misty trail of blood behind him.

I reached the edge and looked down, expecting to see Luke's body, whether wolf or human, but instead all I saw was blood-stained water.

"You little bastard!" With that as my only warning, I was hauled to my feet by Baldy. The gun was still in his hand, and while he held me with his other hand in my hair, he swept the gun about, searching for Luke.

He swung around at a ripple from the far end of the pool, and pulled the trigger three times in rapid succession. Before he could fire again, I brought my bound hands up and smacked his arm. The next bullet shattered one of the plate glass windows. The gun was an old Webley Revolver, so that meant there was only one more bullet in the six round cylinder.

"I've just about had enough of you," Baldy declared, and turned the gun on me. His face was blotchy red with anger as he raised the hand holding the gun, then brought it down sharply. The butt of the revolver connected with my temple, and my vision swam in and out of focus.

He still had a tight grip on my hair, and pushed me to the ground before dropping to his knees beside me. There was pain in my head, and I couldn't make my body respond to the simplest commands. Nor could I understand why it was suddenly difficult to breathe, until I realised that my head was under the water. I struggled, but the more I thrashed the tighter his grip became on my hair.

Physically restrained and compromised, my senses dulled, my mind began to throw out images of family and friends, childhood pets and favoured toys. *Luke.* The beat of my heart, the pulse of blood in my veins, a contagious smile, the fire of arousal. He was all that and more. Luke. *My mate.*

I felt more than heard the roar that seemed to shake the ground, and in the next second I was free. Coughing and spluttering, I heaved myself out of the pool and collapsed onto the tile, blinking water from my eyes. My lungs burned when I breathed, but I levered myself up onto my elbows and looked around me.

Luke, somewhere between wolf and human form, stood tall and magnificent on hind legs, arms stretched out under impossibly wide shoulders, and head thrown back as he howled his outrage. He dropped to all fours then, and sprang forwards, covering the distance from the end of the pool to where I lay in bare seconds.

"Oh my God," Victor Doubleday whispered, watching with wide eyes, apparently immobilised as Luke bore down on him. His men fled for the door, pushing and shoving each other in their efforts to get out first. He cast his gaze around frantically, then dived towards something, only to be beaten to the gun Baldy had dropped by Andy.

Luke lashed out at Doubleday, using the back of his paw to send the man flying into the pool. Had he used his claws, I was certain Doubleday would have landed in pieces. Luke then turned on Andy, but the detective trained the gun on him. He was trembling, but he was so close to Luke that there was little chance he would miss if he pulled the trigger.

"You," Andy said, pointing to me with his free hand. "Get up and come over here."

Luke snarled and moved to stand in front of me. He was all suppressed energy and latent power.

I got to my feet unsteadily—too many damn hits to the head in one day—and stepped out from behind Luke. There was a six inch long gash in his side, and it was bleeding freely. Shouldn't his super-healing thing be kicking in already?

"We both know there's only one bullet left in that gun, Andy," I said, moving slowly towards him. "If you use it to kill me, Luke will tear you to shreds. If you kill *him*, I will make it my life's mission to destroy you."

"You've already destroyed me," Andy screamed, gripping the gun so tightly that his hand shook. "Do you know what it's like to lose your family in one fell swoop?"

I shook my head. "No, no I don't. But Luke does. People like Doubleday tore everyone he loved from him when he was just sixteen." I took another step, until I was equidistant between Luke and Andy.

"I don't give a shit about Luke," Andy replied, mouth twisted. "Maybe Doubleday was right about him and his kind. How is *that* natural?"

"Will that be how you justify killing him to yourself?" I asked. "He's never done anything to hurt you. You could leave now and we wouldn't be able to stop you."

"I'm not leaving without you." Andy waved the gun to gesture me forwards.

At the exact same moment I heard it in my head. "*Down.*" Luke's voice, reverberating with concern, hope, and determination.

I dropped without thought, hitting the tile hard and snapping my head back to see what was going on above me, peripherally aware of Doubleday splashing around in the pool.

As soon as I was clear, Luke's arm shot out and the syringe flew across the space between him and Andy to lodge itself in the soft skin of the detective's inner wrist. Andy emitted a shocked gasp, and reflexively dropped the gun. I wasted no time scrambling forwards, but with my own wrists still tightly bound, my fingers were starting to go numb, making it hard to grip the revolver. Instead I swung at it and sent it skidding across the floor, out of anyone's reach.

Cursing mightily, Andy pulled the syringe—which Luke had emptied—from his arm, tossed it aside and paused for only a second before rushing for the door. A second, it turned out, was too long. Luke was too fast, too strong...too everything. He had Andy pinned to the floor before the man was even over the threshold.

I sensed Luke's rage, and my own panic flared to life again. I couldn't let him kill Andy—he would never forgive himself for taking a life.

"Luke, please, *no.*" I shuffled onto my knees, but found that I could get no farther. Exhaustion and the pain of my injuries stole the last of my energy, and I simply slumped there, begging him silently to *"stop, please stop"*.

When his spine stiffened, I knew I'd got through to him. He rose smoothly, dragging Andy up with him. Andy looked paler than the moon, and when Luke leaned in and *roared* in his face, the detective fainted dead away.

Luke lowered him to the floor, then turned to me. He slit the tape around my wrists with one sharp claw, then shifted back to his human form and dropped to his knees in front of me and lifted his hands to my face but seemed afraid to touch me.

"I'm okay," I assured him, peeling the tape off and flexing my fingers until they tingled with returning sensation. "You came for me. You were going to give up your life for mine."

He looked endearingly puzzled, head tilted to the side, frowning. "Of course."

Of course, just like that. I lifted my hand and punched him on the shoulder. "Don't ever do it again. And put some bloody clothes on."

Laughing softly, but with obvious joy, he leant forward and touched his forehead to mine. "So this is how it feels to have a wish come true."

"A wish?" I asked, curling my fingers around his and bringing them to rest on his thigh.

I felt rather than saw his smile. "I wished for a mate who would challenge me, who wouldn't bow to me."

Tired laughter worked its way up from my chest, but it faltered when I felt the drip of his blood as it landed on my hand. "You're still bleeding," I said, rather unnecessarily, and ducked down to look at the wound in his side.

"It's just a graze," Luke reassured, kissing the top of my head. "It will take longer to heal because the bullet was silver, but it *will* heal. I'll likely have a scar though. I'm told scars are sexy."

I shook my head and shivered at the sight of his blood on my hand. "Not when they're on someone you love."

"Dear God," Luke said breathlessly. "If there wasn't a bedraggled old man about to slip out through that broken window, I would have you right here."

"What?" I turned and saw that Victor Doubleday was indeed about to escape through the broken window. I tried to push myself to my feet, but Luke's hand on my shoulder stopped me.

"Don't worry, he won't get far." With a surprising lack of concern, he grabbed the clothes that he'd shed when he'd shifted and quickly redressed himself, then helped me to get up from the floor.

"What about Detective Andy?" I asked, happy to let Luke take most of my weight. We stepped over the prone man, and headed for the front door. We were just a few feet from it when the door burst open, and there was DCI Ken Trask and Detective Sergeant Matt Bennett.

As soon as they saw us they lowered their guns and rushed forwards. Behind them I could just make out Victor Doubleday being hustled into a police van by Georgie and a uniformed officer.

Matt reached out to lend a hand, but Luke quickly shook his head. "I've got Hal, you'd better deal with your colleague."

"Andy?" Ken asked, voice thick with concern when he saw his fallen colleague. "What the hell is he doing here?"

"He was working with Doubleday," Luke growled. "He's responsible for what happened to Hal, and he's lucky I didn't rip out his fucking throat." Without waiting for a reply, he led me out into the cold November afternoon.

"A blanket and an ambulance," Luke commanded of a young uniformed officer who immediately ran to comply.

Georgie came over to us and led us to an unmarked car, where she opened the back door for me to sit while I awaited my ambulance. On the way, I got a look in the back of the police van, and saw Victor Doubleday had joined his three henchmen, the four of them cuffed and staring silently ahead.

I wasn't alone in the car. On the front passenger seat, wrapped in an orange blanket, Milo glanced back over his shoulder and smiled sheepishly.

"Milo?" Luke crouched down beside me, rested his hands on my knees, and squinted in surprise at Milo. "I told you to stay at home."

"I know, I know, but I couldn't sit there and do nothing," the boy exclaimed, wide-eyed.

"So, you did what, instead?" Luke asked.

"I…" Milo lowered his eyes. "I know they said you couldn't contact the police, but I'm not you, so technically… I called Detective Trask and told him I could shift and follow your scent."

Luke's fingers tightened on my knees and he uttered an unintelligible sound that somehow managed to convey shock and disbelief. "Are you telling me that you ran through the streets of London while shifted, in *broad daylight*?"

"I guess people thought they were just seeing a dog." Milo shrugged, cheeks colouring. "I let the detective put a collar with a tracker on me."

Luke sighed and shook his head. "I don't know whether to be proud or to kick your arse for putting yourself at risk like that. We'll talk about this later."

Nodding, but not looking too worried, Milo turned his attention to me. "Are you okay, Hal?"

I smiled, and winced when I felt it in my split lip. "I'm better now." My body ached like I'd been run over by a steam roller, my head was throbbing, one of my eyes had swollen shut and the taste of my own blood was making me feel queasy, but with Milo there in front of me and Luke at my side, gently rubbing my wrists, his scent filling my nostrils, I actually *did* feel better. Better than better, even.

* * * *

At the request of the doctor—and Luke's vehement insistence—I remained in hospital overnight, and after being poked, prodded and generally manhandled, I was allowed the bliss of a soft bed, a private room, and a handy button to self-administer pain medication.

When his own injury was treated, Luke took a seat at the side of my bed and refused, point blank, to move all night. Ken Trask took Milo back to stay with his family for the night, and when Luke and I arrived back at Luke's place the following afternoon, Milo and Ken were waiting for us.

"You're looking very pleased with yourself, Detective," I noted as I eased into a chair at the kitchen table. "Milo, be a sweetheart and make me some tea?"

The boy smiled and went to fill the kettle. Luke took the seat beside me. I didn't miss the troubled glance he gave me—I guess I must have looked like one of Frankenstein's earlier efforts, with all my bruises coming into full-bloom. I laid a hand on his knee, as much for myself as for him.

"I have a lot to be happy about today," Ken replied, sitting across from us. "We have Robert Doubleday bang to rights after finding the bodies at the farm and matching the bullet used to kill one with his gun. With Victor in jail we've effectively cut the head off the Prime Order snake, and their confederates are queuing up to testify against them in hope of cutting a deal. I swear to God, I thought the Home Secretary was going to give me a lap dance, he was so happy."

I snorted at that, and grimaced at the pain in my ribs. I thought of Baldy and Buzz-cut and wished them every pleasantry Her Majesty's prison service could offer.

"We're hoping for a February date for the trials to begin," Ken said.

"I can think of no better Valentine gift than seeing the Doubledays in the dock together." I grinned.

"I can," Luke rumbled, and I looked over to see him watching me with that oh so familiar heat in his eyes. In spite of the tortures my body had been through, I responded with Pavlovian speed. Desire raced through my veins and my groin—ironically the only part of me that *didn't* hurt—tightened with a very different kind of ache.

"Will the guards still be around the house?" Milo asked, setting a mug down in front of me and resting his hand on my shoulder in an endearingly protective manner.

Ken nodded. "I'm afraid so. You're okay to stay here, aren't you, Milo?"

"Uh, yes, I suppose...if it's okay with Luke and Hal?" He sounded so uncertain that I would have hugged him if I was a lover of physical pain. Instead, I squeezed Luke's thigh.

"Of course it's okay," Luke said, sounding surprised that there was any question.

Had he not been standing right beside me I probably wouldn't have heard Milo's sigh of relief. I lifted my free hand and patted his.

"What will happen to Andy?" I asked, and felt both Luke and Milo tense.

Ken's smile disappeared, replaced with a deep frown. "He'll be tried for abduction and conspiracy to commit murder."

A cold hand clutched at my heart. Murder. *Holy fuck, they were really going to kill us.* It only hit me in that moment, and I took a sip of tea to cover up the whimper that I'm certain was working its way from my chest.

"He's lucky to be alive," Luke declared, and I had a sudden sensation of fear and anguish that wasn't my own. It was…humbling and exciting to be so in tune with Luke.

"I want to apologise," Ken said, shaking his head as if he still couldn't quite believe it. "But it seems so bloody inadequate after everything."

"It wasn't your fault, Ken, there was no way you could have known," I said, feeling sorry for him.

He continued to shake his head. "I should have known about his family connection to John Stoke at the very least. I can assure you that I will be seriously beefing up my unit's security."

"Mmm, beef, I could really go for a big juicy steak about now," I said, licking my lips as the craving came over me.

Luke snorted, Milo chuckled and Ken smiled, getting to his feet. He glanced between Luke and me and nodded. "Right, I'll get out of your hair for now. But remember, my wife still wants you all over for that dinner, and Milo, Josh wants a re-match in *Call of Duty*."

"Josh?" I asked, as Luke showed Ken out.

"Detective Trask's older son. He's pretty cool," Milo said too casually, though his cheeks pinkened and he didn't meet my eyes.

"Okay, then," Luke said, rubbing his hands together. "Steak for three"—he looked at Milo who nodded his assent—"I'll get that started as soon as you're settled in bed."

"Bed? Why do I have to go to bed?" I'm not ashamed to admit that I sounded like a whiny child.

Luke arched an eyebrow and held out his hands. "The doctor said lots of rest for a few days, so it's dinner, breakfast and lunch in bed for you."

Taking his hands, I allowed him to ease me up out of my seat, unable to suppress a moan.

"I'll bring you some more tea," Milo said, and it was official—I was being ganged up on.

I grinned and went slowly upstairs with Luke.

I refused to actually get into bed, but toed off my shoes and lay back against the pile of pillows Luke fluffed up, still dressed and on top of the duvet. "Come and sit beside me," I said, wiggling my fingers at Luke.

Kicking off his own shoes, he got onto the bed and propped himself up beside me. He wanted to hold me, I felt the need in him, but I also felt his caution and resistance—he was afraid of hurting me. I took one of his hands between both of mine and held it to my heart.

"I got a message from the property agent, I can buy the house. Come and live with me," he said, voice rough with emotion. "Not just until the trial is over, but forever."

He must have felt the way my heart flipped over in my chest. I nodded. "Yes. Forever."

The smile he gave me was breathtaking.

"And, I was thinking," he added, a little hesitantly. "About Milo. There's a flat over the garage, it's completely self-contained. I was thinking that, when this is all over, he might like to live there—it would give him all the independence he needs, and he'd still have us close by."

I nodded, fighting the sting of tears. "I think that sounds wonderful. I'll tell Mum to expect one more for Christmas dinner."

"What about our security detail?" Luke asked, pleasure lighting his pale blue eyes.

"Mum will find it all vastly exciting, and Dad probably won't notice." I reached up and pulled his head down to mine for a brief kiss, needing his closeness.

"My Hal," Luke whispered, a world of feeling in the two syllables.

My breath hitched and I ran my fingers through his thick, blond hair. "My beautiful white wolf. My *mate*." I kissed him again, tasting him, breathing his air, and felt him tremble against me.

We broke apart only when we heard Milo's footsteps in the hall.

"How about I light a fire in the grate, and we eat dinner together in here and watch a movie?" Luke asked.

I nodded, unable to speak for the emotion clogging my throat. After putting my tea on the night table, Milo snagged the big armchair by the window. "I vote for *Die Hard 4*."

Groaning, I said, "How about something a little less…punishing?"

Milo flushed, expression all apology. "*Harry Potter*?"

"Perfect!" I grinned, and turned my gaze to Luke. Just perfect.

Our path to this point had been less than smooth, and I suspected we had a few rocky moments ahead, but I wouldn't have changed one stumbling footstep for anything.

About the Author

A devourer of books since the age of three, Cassidy Ryan has wanted to be a writer since she discovered that actual people created these wonderful worlds and characters.

She discovered her mum's stash of romance novels when she was twelve, and the die was cast.

These days she lives in the West End of Glasgow, and when she isn't meeting the demands of her cat Angel—the undisputed Mistress of all She Surveys—or indulging in her life-long quest to find the perfect handbag, she likes nothing better than to sit down at the laptop and manoeuvre gorgeous men and women into bed, in whatever combination the muse sees fit to gift upon her imagination.

Cassidy Ryan loves to hear from readers. You can find her contact information, website details and author profile page at http://www.total-e-bound.com.

Total-E-Bound Publishing

www.total-e-bound.com

Take a look at our exciting range of literagasmic™
erotic romance titles and discover pure quality
at Total-E-Bound.